"What do you think you're playing at?"

Kate swallowed nervously. "I'm not playing at anything. I'm simply asking you not to kiss me again."

Luke swore under his breath, his face turned to granite. "Are you trying to tell me," he said in a low angry voice, "that you didn't enjoy what we did just now?"

Kate blinked. If she told him the truth, that she had enjoyed it, he would try to carry on where they had left off, and she knew instinctively that that path led to heartache. If she told him a lie he would be very, very angry. She took a deep breath.

"I didn't enjoy it," she whispered, looking him straight in the eye and hoping she sounded convincing.

Through tightly clamped teeth he growled, "You lying little tease!"

WELCOME
TO THE WONDERFUL WORLD
OF *Harlequin Presents*

Interesting, informative and entertaining,
each Harlequin Romance portrays an appealing
and original love story. With a varied array
of settings, we may lure you on an African safari,
to a quaint Welsh village, or an exotic Riviera
location—anywhere and everywhere that adventurous
men and women fall in love.

As publishers of Harlequin Romances, we're
extremely proud of our books. Since 1949,
Harlequin Enterprises has built its publishing
reputation on the solid base of quality and
originality. Our stories are the most popular
paperback romances sold in North America; every
month, six new titles are released and sold at
nearly every book-selling store in Canada and the
United States.

A free catalogue listing all Harlequin Romances
can be yours by writing to the

HARLEQUIN READER SERVICE,
(In the U.S.) 1440 South Priest Drive, Tempe, AZ 85281
(In Canada) Stratford, Ontario, Canada N5A 6W2

We sincerely hope you enjoy reading
this Harlequin Romance.

Yours truly,

THE PUBLISHERS
Harlequin Romances

SARAH HOLLAND

too hot to handle

Harlequin Books

TORONTO · LONDON · LOS ANGELES · AMSTERDAM
SYDNEY · HAMBURG · PARIS · STOCKHOLM · ATHENS · TOKYO

For
GUDI
(and her sisters)

Harlequin Presents edition published July 1982
ISBN 0-373-10516-9

Original hardcover edition published in 1982
by Mills & Boon Limited

CHAPTER ONE

KATE recognised him immediately. He stood in the orange glow of the street light, beside a sleek, low-slung sports car. He was talking in a deep voice to two other men as they stood outside a house from which music and voices floated through the night.

His electric blue eyes glittered wickedly in the lamp light, his tanned face arrogantly sensual. His body was lithe, and powerfully muscled, every movement he made stamped with naked sexuality. He was taller than she had expected, towering over his companions. A slight breeze lifted his jet-black hair softly, his eyes were narrowed against the sudden cold.

Luke Hastings was featured prominently in the gossip columns. His dark, arrogant face stared broodingly out of the pages of glossy magazines. Conjecture about his private life surrounded him. He was an enigma, taking care to stay out of the glare of the spotlight when he was off stage.

His dark, melodic voice could be heard almost any time of day on radio stations all over the world. The lyrics and the exquisitely beautiful melodies of his songs inspired and moved anyone who listened to them. He was the most prolific, sought-after singer on both sides of the Atlantic.

'Imagine seeing Luke Hastings in the flesh!' whispered Linda in an excited voice beside her.

Kate glanced at her with ill-concealed irritation.

They were on their way back from the office Christmas party. It had been boring as usual. Kate was tired. All she wanted to do was go home and go to sleep. She didn't want to stand around and gaze at Luke Hastings.

She turned to look at her friend. 'Let's go home,' she suggested with a tired smile.

Linda peered at her crossly. She was too vain to wear her glasses, and had a disconcerting habit of screwing up her eyes and peering at people as though she was trying to look right through them.

'Oh, Kate,' she wheedled, her face pleading, 'we can't turn up a chance like this!'

'You may not be able to,' Kate told her, eyeing her drily, 'but I think I'll survive.' She took her arm and began to steer her across the road and away from Luke Hastings.

Linda shook her arm free. 'I want to get his autograph,' she hissed, 'I want to talk to him.'

Kate sighed. If only they had taken a taxi from the station! But their monthly pay cheque didn't quite stretch to that. She looked at the man by the car. From the odds and ends she had read about him, he didn't exactly welcome publicity. Linda was determined to make them both look like school-girls—excited and adoring.

'It would be too embarrassing,' she said.

Linda pouted like a child and stared at her accusingly. Kate could see that Linda was going to be impossible. No doubt she would sulk for days on end if Kate didn't relent. Linda was an experienced sulker. She liked getting her own way.

'Spoilsport!' Linda hissed, tossing her blonde curls

and turning up her nose, her round blue eyes boring accusingly into Kate's.

It was pointless to argue. Kate sighed again and shrugged slim shoulders. 'Very well. But I'm not coming with you. If you want to get his autograph, you go and get it. I'll stay here.'

Linda glared at her. 'But I don't want to go on my own.'

Kate regarded her with growing impatience. Any minute now, Linda would put her tongue out and stamp her foot, and Kate wouldn't be in the least bit surprised if she did. It was like living with a ten-year-old at times.

'That's too bad,' she told her firmly. 'I'm not coming with you, and that is final.'

Linda scowled in the darkness, her pretty, heart-shaped face taking on a sulky look. Kate knew it only too well. If she didn't give in, Linda would sulk for days, making life practically impossible in the flat. She decided that peace was preferable to endless sulking and banging of doors.

'Oh, all right,' she said on a sigh.

Linda beamed, becoming sweet and grateful in a matter of seconds. She fished out her mirror and patted her curls, vain to the last. Kate looked down at her camel coat, belted tightly at the waist. It wasn't particularly glamorous, she admitted with a grimace, but it was warm and comfortable.

They walked towards the car, and Luke Hastings looked up at their approach. He smiled lazily, ex-posing strong, white teeth, vivid against his tanned skin. He was devastatingly attractive at such close quarters.

Linda gazed at him in awe, her eyes over-bright. 'Are you Luke Hastings?' she asked in an excited voice.

'Yes,' he replied in a deep tone, his eyes rakishly amused, 'I'm Luke Hastings.'

'I'm so pleased to meet you,' Linda gushed, 'I'd love to have your autograph. If you don't mind, that is.'

The meek shall inherit the earth, Kate thought drily, watching Linda as she gazed adoringly at him.

Luke's blue eyes flickered over to Kate, amusement in their depths as he took the pen and paper from Linda. Kate compressed her lips. Linda was worse than she had expected.

Luke leaned back against the side of the black car. 'Who's it for?' he asked in a casual voice.

Linda leaned forwards slightly. 'If you could just write "For Linda" that would be lovely,' she gushed happily.

'For Linda,' he murmured, writing in bold strokes. He raised one jet-black eyebrow in Kate's direction, his gaze sweeping over her pale, oval face framed with thick, glossy black hair, and finally fixing on her large, luminous, peppermint green eyes. 'What's your name?' he asked softly.

'Kate,' she answered automatically, slightly puzzled.

'Kate,' he repeated in a dark, sexy voice, smiling as he began to write once more. 'For Kate, with all my love,' he murmured as he wrote.

'I don't want your autograph,' she blurted out. 'It was Linda who wanted it, not me.' She stopped, realising how rude it must have sounded.

He raised his well-shaped black head slowly. 'I see.' His eyes held hers.

'I didn't mean it like that,' she began hastily, tripping over the words as she caught a glimpse of amusement in his eyes. Damn Linda! Why did she have to come over and ask for his wretched autograph?

His mouth twitched at the corners as he watched her, and Kate's lips compressed with anger. He was laughing at her! It was typical of Linda to land her in a situation like this.

'She doesn't really mean it, do you, Kate?' Linda nudged her warningly, her brow marred by an anxious frown. Kate glared at her. Now she had made it worse.

'Of course not,' she mumbled in a stilted voice.

Luke smiled and handed her the piece of paper. Kate's fingers were stiff as she took it from him, and she controlled a desire to hit him.

'Thank you,' she muttered.

At that moment, a car pulled up opposite them and four men got out. Luke Hastings turned to look at them, and the expression on his face turned from one of amusement to one of irritation, his eyes narrowing angrily. He turned to the men still standing beside him.

'I'll call you on Monday,' he told them, taking a set of keys from his pocket and beginning to open the car door.

Kate turned to Linda, feeling relieved. 'Let's go home,' she said quietly.

Linda was not pleased. She scowled. 'Give that to me,' she said, snatching the autograph from Kate.

But she dropped it, and it fluttered to the ground, and Luke's foot came down on it. Linda wailed, bending to pick it up.

She pushed at Luke's foot, and he turned to look down at the muddy paper. He gave a sigh of exasperation and bent to pick it up, knocking Kate off balance as he did so.

Kate felt herself fall sideways, her hipbone connecting with the car door with a sickening thud. She tried to regain her balance, but her ankle twisted painfully and she felt herself begin to topple backwards. A light flashed in the dark street.

A strong pair of arms caught and held her. She looked up dazedly into electric blue eyes, smelt the heady male scent of him as another light went off, illuminating them in each other's arms.

She heard him swear under his breath as he turned to look at the men coming towards them. She turned, feeling dazed and puzzled, then she saw the camera one of the men carried.

'Thanks, Luke!' shouted the photographer cheerfully. 'Let's have some more like that!'

Luke's teeth snapped together in anger, then he looked at Kate. Her hipbone was throbbing and her ankle hurt. She stared back at him.

'Damn,' he muttered, opening the car door and pushing her inside. Kate gaped at Linda, who stood on the pavement, gaping back at her.

Luke was quickly in the seat beside her as the reporters arrived by the car. The photographer was clicking away merrily as Luke started the car, and Kate stared in horrified amazement as the car began to pull away.

'Kate!' she heard Linda's shocked voice above the noise the men were making.

Kate thumped her hands on the window. She pushed at the door handle, but it wouldn't move. She watched Linda disappear slowly into the distance as they drove away down the dark street.

Kate swallowed noiselessly. Now what was she going to do? She looked at Luke. His face was set angrily, and fear crept into her stomach. She was going to have a little word with Linda when she finally got home. If she got home. The thought occurred to her with a jolt. She eyed Luke warily, and moved closer to the door.

'Where do you live?' His voice was crisp and clear, but he didn't turn to look at her.

'We've passed it, actually,' Kate told him weakly.

He glanced at her. 'I didn't ask you that. I asked where you lived.'

Her lips tightened. She gave her address stiffly and watched as he wordlessly turned the car around, his strong, tanned hand closing over the gear stick, the gold watch he wore peeping out from beneath crisp white cuff and black jacket sleeve.

Kate pressed a tentative hand to her ankle. It was still throbbing. There would be a nasty bruise there in the morning.

He glanced down at her, his eyes skimming over the long slim legs visible below the hem of her silky red dress. 'How does it feel?'

Kate eyed him with irritation. 'It hurts.'

A frown marred his brow. 'Do you think it's badly hurt?'

Kate pressed the bone gingerly, feeling for signs of a crack. 'No, I don't think so. It's probably just bruised.'

'Would you like me to take a look?'

'No, thank you,' Kate said primly, taking her hand away from her ankle and sitting up straight.

He smiled but said nothing in reply. Kate looked out of the window as they pulled up outside her flat. Luke leaned back in his seat, watching as she rummaged in her bag for her keys. Her heart dropped like a stone. Linda had the keys! When they went out together, they only took one set of keys, and Linda had them.

She looked up at the first floor flat. No lights were on. Linda should easily have been home now; they had only been a hundred yards away when Luke had bundled her into the car.

Kate bit her lip anxiously and stepped out of the car, saying goodnight to Luke. She walked up to the front door and pressed the bell. Nothing happened. The sound of the bell echoed through the empty flat.

She turned and waved brightly to Luke, hoping he would go away, but he didn't move, and the engine continued running as he watched and waited. Kate rang the bell again, leaving her finger on it for a long time. But nothing happened.

'Come on, Linda,' she muttered under her breath. Luke's presence was unnerving. Why didn't he just go away?

The flat was still silent. Where on earth was Linda? Kate sighed and stepped back, bending to pick up a small stone from the garden. She aimed it for the front window, and it hit the centre of the glass panel, falling back to the ground with a hollow sound. Kate searched anxiously for a sign of Linda's blonde head at the window of her bedroom.

Fear began to creep back into her stomach. She didn't like the prospect of sitting on the doorstep, locked out all night, alone in the middle of London. Her heart began to beat faster with anxiety.

The silence was broken as Luke switched off the car engine. The door opened and shut, and his footsteps came towards her. She turned around, feeling very stupid.

He towered over her. 'Nobody home?' he asked, one black brow raised as he looked at her.

She shook her head helplessly, looking back at the window. If only she had brought her keys with her!

'Why didn't you tell me you didn't have your keys?' Luke asked, sliding one hand into the pocket of his black trousers.

She eyed him. 'You didn't ask.'

'That's hardly the point,' he said drily, his gaze skimming over her slender figure encased in the beige coat.

Kate sighed, looking back up at the window, still hoping that Linda's head would somehow miraculously appear. 'I don't see that it makes much difference,' she told him with a shrug.

Luke followed her gaze. 'I take it you're on the first floor,' he commented.

Kate's ankle was hurting. She sat down on the stone wall surrounding the big old house. 'Yes,' she told him. 'That's Linda's bedroom at the front.' She buried her hands deeper in the pockets of her coat.

It was getting colder the more she stood around without moving.

'Is it just the two of you?' Luke asked.

Kate nodded vaguely. She was worried about Linda. There was no sign of her along the darkened street, and she obviously wasn't in the flat. The bell was very loud—she wouldn't miss it if she was in.

'Any idea where she might have gone?' Luke asked, his voice deep and crisp.

She shook her head miserably. 'No, we only moved in here a couple of weeks ago. We don't really know anyone near here.'

'So you couldn't wake any of the neighbours,' he pointed out, almost to himself.

Kate smiled faintly, in spite of the mood which was beginning to settle over her. 'Not unless I want to make some enemies.'

Luke took out a case from his inside jacket pocket and lit a cigar, watching as the silver-blue smoke was blown away almost immediately by the winter breeze. 'I don't suppose any windows are open?' he asked casually.

'No.' Her voice was miserable and a little hopeless. 'We always make a point of locking everything before we come out.' She had lived at home with her parents previously, and a flat of her own was a responsibility she didn't want to fall down on.

'Do you know anyone you can ring up and stay with for the night?' He watched her steadily with those penetrating blue eyes as he spoke.

She shook her head again. 'Not really. I only started working at this office a month ago. I don't know anyone well enough to ring them up at this time of night.'

Luke frowned, his face thoughtful. He drew on his cigar and looked back at Kate. 'How's your ankle?'

Kate looked down at her foot in surprise. The worry had made her forget her pain for a moment. 'It doesn't hurt so much now,' she admitted.

'Shall I take a look at it for you?'

Kate shook her head quickly. 'No, thank you. I'm sure it'll be all right.'

Luke moved closer to where she sat, his eyes glittering, a smile on his face. 'Are you sure?'

Kate stood up on unsteady legs. There was something indefinable about this man that unnerved her, made her feel small and helpless beside his obvious strength. 'Quite sure,' she told him firmly. He was having a very strange effect on her.

He shrugged. 'So what happens now?'

'I don't know,' Kate replied, her fears returning in a rush. 'I suppose I'll just have to wait until she comes home.'

A frown marred his brow. 'Don't you think that might be dangerous?'

She pushed her hands deeper into her coat pockets, watching her breath steam up in front of her, and shrugged. 'I don't see that I have much choice,' she pointed out.

'You do realise,' he said softly, moving closer to her, 'that I can help you out?'

Kate backed away from him, putting up a hand to wave him away. 'Oh, that's really not necessary,' she said, her voice breathless, afraid of what he was going to suggest.

His eyes glittered wickedly. 'It's the least I can do,' he murmured.

Kate shook her head. 'I'll be all right,' she stammered, feeling the cold wall of the house against her back. She pressed against the wall, staring wide-eyed at Luke as he moved closer.

He reached out one long, sinewy hand and captured her chin, tilting it upwards, the blue eyes focussing on hers.

'After all,' he said in a husky voice, 'I must help you in some way. I got you into this situation.'

'That's quite all right,' she babbled. 'It's all forgotten now.'

His gaze flickered down to her mouth, then back to her eyes, and he took her arm in a gentle movement. 'Come with me,' he murmured against her silky black hair.

'Where are we going?' Kate asked desperately.

He smiled, his eyes twinkling. 'To look for your friend, of course. Where did you think we were going?'

Kate's lips tightened angrily. Infuriating man! she thought, glaring at him as he opened the car door for her. He smiled at her as he slid in the seat beside her, and Kate threw him a vicious look, resisting the desire to sink her teeth in his hand.

They pulled away from the kerb, driving slowly through the dimly lit streets. Kate stared out of the window, searching for a sign of Linda, but she was nowhere to be seen.

Luke turned the car around, his thighs rippling beneath the black material as he depressed the clutch. Kate averted her eyes in disgust. He even looks sexy driving a car, she thought crossly, is there nothing wrong with him?

After touring the area thoroughly, they returned to her flat, pulling up outside in a heavy silence.

'Try the bell again,' Luke told her as he leaned back in his seat. 'She may have returned while we've been gone.'

Kate walked up to the front door and pressed the bell. Nothing happened. Linda was definitely not in. She sighed, feeling near to tears. What on earth was she to do? Where was Linda?

She walked back to the car, feeling lost, and very miserable.

'Still not in?' Luke asked gently.

Kate shook her head. It was such a ridiculous situation to be in that she had a feeling she ought to see the funny side of it. But she had never felt less like laughing.

What on earth could she do now? She had nowhere to spend the night. Her family lived too far away, in the heart of Essex, for her to drive down to them. She didn't know any of the girls in her office well enough, and she didn't think she really knew where they lived.

The thought of Brian occurred to her momentarily, but she dismissed the idea. She had only been seeing him for a fortnight, and although she had safely resisted his advances up until now, she had her doubts about him. She had got the message over to him that she wasn't the sort of girl to sleep with her boy-friends. He had accepted her honesty, and appeared to respect her for it. But people can be deceptive, and she didn't want to spend an evening fighting him off.

Luke drummed long, tanned fingers on the steering wheel. His eyes held hers as he watched her. 'There's only one thing you can do now,' he told her in a soft voice.

She eyed him warily. 'What's that?'

He smiled, and his face was transformed with the devastating charm of that smile. 'You'll have to come home with me.'

She stared at him. She didn't trust that charming smile. 'No,' she told him firmly. 'Oh, no!'

'Don't be absurd. You have very little choice.'

'No,' she repeated stubbornly.

Luke watched her, his black head tilted to one side. 'Am I such a frightening prospect?' he asked gently.

Kate regarded him with unblinking eyes. Honesty, she decided, was definitely the best policy. 'Yes.'

'I don't know what you've read about me,' he said slowly, 'but I'm not the wolf the media would have everyone believe.'

Her eyebrows rose with evident disbelief. 'You look extremely wolf-like to me!'

He laughed softly, shaking his head with amusement. His gaze flickered over her face caressingly, almost as though he hadn't before noticed quite how beautiful the girl at his side was. Her deep, wide green eyes stared up at him like oval peppermints set in a pale, translucent skin framed with long, silky black hair.

Kate remembered reading an article which had said that Luke was tired of the false, brittle women he met. He despised the tinsel and glitter of the world in which he worked, and tried to steer clear of it as much as possible.

Luke smiled at her. 'You don't seriously think I'm going to drive off and leave you alone on your door-step?'

'I was hoping you would, actually,' Kate told him. His presence in the car was overwhelming. His body was so powerful, and so very close to hers. She huddled nervously in her side of the car.

'Why?' he asked calmly.

'Because I don't trust you.' Her voice came out weak and uncertain.

The black brows jerked together in surprise. 'Surely you'd feel safer with me than with a perfect stranger who came along to find you sitting alone on your doorstep?'

Kate shrugged. 'That's a chance I'll just have to take,' she said, trying to sound firm. She pushed at the door handle. It didn't move, so she tried it again, frowning. It still didn't move.

Her head swung round. 'What have you done to the door?' she demanded, her eyes wide with sudden fear.

He watched her calmly. 'I've locked it.'

Her lips tightened. 'I can see that,' she said, her stomach beginning to churn. 'Open the door at once and let me out!'

Luke ignored her, inserting the keys in the ignition and starting the car. Kate pushed frantically at the door handle, then banged her fists against the window.

'Open the door!' she wailed, her voice rising as fear began to get a grip on her.

The car pulled away smoothly from the kerb. 'Sit

down in your seat and stop getting hysterical,' Luke told her in a calm voice, his eyes fixed on the road ahead of them.

Kate blinked in disbelief. She was being driven off against her will by a stranger! She swallowed and looked at him.

'Will you please open the door and let me out?' she croaked, her throat dry and tight with nerves.

'I've told you, just sit back and relax. I'll put you up for the night,' he told her firmly.

'But I don't want you to,' she protested. 'I'd much rather sit and wait for Linda to come home.' God only knew what was on his mind. From what she had read about him, Luke Hastings was a womaniser. She didn't want to become another scalp on his belt.

Luke turned to her, his face holding intense irritation. 'You've been just as much trouble to me as I have to you, you stupid girl. Now would you just sit still and stop arguing!'

Kate glared at him, her hands curling into fists. 'If I've been so much trouble to you, why did you bundle me into the car in the first place?'

He sighed, the heavy-lidded eyes closing momentarily. 'Because those reporters picked up a good story with pictures to go with it. If I'd driven off and left you after all that happened, what conclusion do you think they would have drawn?'

Kate saw his point. She would have been pictured as the deserted, not to mention battered woman— not exactly what one wants to read over breakfast.

'Do you suppose they'll print it?' she asked dismally.

'They usually do.'

Kate sighed. It looked as though she was going to get a lot more than she had bargained for by giving in to Linda's request. Far from having peace, her whole day had been turned upside down and given a good shake.

But the newspaper story was one of her lesser worries. The main thing on her mind was how to get out of the car and away from Luke. She looked at him, her eyes tracing the commanding profile, the hard-boned face, strong, assertive jawline.

'I don't suppose you'd consider taking me back to my flat?' she asked hopefully.

'No,' he said with grim amusement, 'I wouldn't.'

Kate glared out of the window with resentment. She was genuinely frightened of Luke, and very, very apprehensive of the coming night. She could handle Brian quite easily, he at least had respect for her principles, but this man appeared to hold no morals or principles at all. How would she handle him if he tried to force her into his bed? She wasn't particularly strong at the best of times, and with a man so obviously powerful as Luke Hastings, she would stand no chance at all.

They pulled up outside a large Georgian-style house in a square. Kate glanced up at the elegant house. 'Is this where you live?' she asked quietly.

'This is it,' he nodded, switching off the engine.

The difference between her way of life and his was instantly recognisable. The house in the elegant square must have cost a figure she wouldn't even care to think of. He was so wealthy and so successful, while she was merely a typist in a publishing firm, earning a small monthly wage, struggling to pay her rent and her bills. What would he expect from her if she went into that house alone with him?

He turned to look at her, his face enigmatic. 'Shall we go in?' he murmured.

Kate swallowed noiselessly, sitting rigidly in her seat, not daring to move.

Luke watched her steadily, his head tilted to one side. He could see how frightened she was, and it puzzled him slightly, because women usually fell over themselves to flirt with him. He wasn't conceited enough to think that they were doing it because they liked his looks or his character. They were generally impressed by his wealth and position. Kate was a refreshing change. She at least was honest, even though it was a slight jolt for his ego.

He leant over, gently taking her hand. 'I won't jump on you, you know,' he told her.

Kate blinked. He didn't really expect her to believe that? She stared straight ahead of her, frightened that he would see the inner turmoil in her eyes if she looked at him.

'Kate?' he asked softly, moving closer to her.

Kate stiffened involuntarily as she felt his breath fan her cheek. Curious sensations stirred inside her as she realised how close his mouth was to her skin. Her heart began to beat faster with panic and excitement. She couldn't distinguish between the two emotions.

Luke shifted slightly, bringing his arm protectively around her, resting his hand lightly on her arm. She felt her breath come faster. His other hand gently stroked her hair, running his long, hard fingers through the silken strands.

'What are you frightened of?' he asked in a soft, deeply seductive voice.

Kate stared straight ahead, her back rigid. His hand left her hair slowly, and he ran one long finger slowly down her cheek, until it reached her lips. He caressed her lips with his finger, opening her mouth slightly as he watched her.

Oh God, she thought desperately, what have I got myself into? She tried to resist the melting feeling his touch was evoking, her bones felt as light as air, but she stubbornly kept herself as unresponsive as possible.

His finger left her lips, his hand capturing her chin gently. He turned her round to face him, her mint-green eyes staring up at him like the eyes of a frightened doe.

'What are you frightened of?' he repeated gently.

Kate stared at him in silence. His face was so close, his firm, sensual lips open slightly, giving a glimpse of strong white teeth. His deep, dazzlingly blue eyes stared broodingly into hers. Her heart was thudding faster, her pulses hammering in her wrists and temples.

It's only because I'm frightened, she told herself wildly. He doesn't attract me. She desperately needed to deny his attraction in case she failed to find the strength with which to fight him off.

'Aren't you going to answer me?' he asked gently.

She couldn't stop staring at his hard mouth as he spoke, seeing how very sensual it was, wondering what it would feel like if her mouth touched his.

Luke sighed, stroking her hair away from her face.

'Kate,' he murmured huskily, his black head coming closer. 'You're so very beautiful.'

His lips touched her cheek, igniting flames as they moved slowly, teasingly to her lips. His mouth met hers softly, brushing backwards and forwards until she felt the breath constrict in her throat.

He coaxed her lips apart, slowly, tantalisingly as she stared at him with wide, confused eyes. Beautiful, exhilarating sensations coursed through her. She didn't know how to cope with this sweet, heated rise of excitement, it was so totally unfamiliar to her.

She kept herself rigid as he kissed her softly, sensually. She felt her bones melting, but refused to allow him to see that far into her heart. She didn't respond, because she didn't know how to, didn't know what dangerous feelings she might arouse in him.

Eventually he lifted his head, his eyes glittering, to look down at her. His breathing was accelerated, his face filled with desire. Kate met his gaze head on.

He released her silently, pressing a button on the dashboard as he moved back into his side of the car. She watched him in disbelief for a moment and their eyes held briefly. Then she turned and fumbled for the doorhandle, stepping out of the car as quickly as she could.

She stood in the cold night air, watching her breath appear in front of her like an eerie mist. Her heart was still thudding, but showed signs of calming down. Her legs felt very weak. She praised herself for her willpower, but also felt a sharp sense of . . . disappointment? No, it couldn't be that.

Luke locked the car and came round to her, taking her arm lightly. They walked up to the front door, and he smiled reassuringly at her. Kate didn't feel in the least reassured. But she stepped bravely over the threshold.

He switched the hall light on, illuminating the tastefully decorated room in all its splendour, and Kate's heart sank into her boots. She averted her eyes from his in the hope that he wouldn't see the fear in them.

The front door closed with a loud click, and she whirled round, jumping with fear.

He looked at her with a sigh of exasperation. 'Stop standing there like a frightened rabbit,' he said, moving past her and up the stairs. 'I'm not in the habit of robbing young girls of their virtue.'

Kate watched him suspiciously, but followed him up the stairs in the end. She had no choice. If she tried to run, he would either follow or leave her to her own devices. She was in no less danger out there than in here with him.

He opened a door off the landing and ushered her in. She looked at it with undisguised pleasure. It was decorated in warm shades of pink and gold, obviously designed with a woman in mind.

'Thank you,' she said. 'It's lovely.'

Luke nodded, but showed no signs of moving from his stance in the doorway.

Kate went nervously towards the door. 'Well, I'll go to bed now,' she said hopefully. 'Goodnight.'

Luke remained where he was. 'Pity you haven't got anything with you to wear for the night,' he remarked with a smile.

Kate's lips compressed. What a fatuous remark! Of course she didn't have anything with her. Then she realised what he meant. She would have to sleep naked. He wouldn't come in, would he? She eyed him warily. He might just do that.

'You don't have anything I could borrow, do you?' she asked in a polite little voice.

Luke smiled with charm. 'Stay there.' He walked down the corridor to a room and appeared a moment later with a pair of black silk pyjamas. 'Here,' he handed them to her. 'I never use them personally,' he announced lazily, and smiled as he saw the blush creep into Kate's face. 'But you know what people are like—I always seem to get a pair for Christmas from someone.'

Kate smiled nervously. 'Thank you, they're very nice,' she said, fingering the black silk with restless hands. She moved over to hold on to the door handle, trying to close it as politely as possible, in his face. 'Well, I'll say goodnight, then.'

He smiled, not moving. 'Goodnight,' he said, his eyes twinkling wickedly.

Kate swallowed, beginning to close the door. Luke's hand snaked out to catch her wrist gently. He leaned forward, his black head coming closer to hers.

'Goodnight, Kate,' he whispered against her lips, brushing them with his hard mouth before drawing away.

Kate felt her heart begin to thud with a mixture of excitement and fear. Was he going to try to seduce her? Or would he leave her to go to sleep on her own?

He watched her for a second in silence, taking in her frightened expression, her wary eyes. Then he pushed away from the doorjamb, moving back into the darkened corridor outside her room. 'Pleasant dreams,' he said softly, and with a sensual smile walked down to his own room.

Kate heaved a sigh of relief and closed the door firmly, locking it from the inside. He wouldn't be able to get in now, so she felt quite safe. She went over to the adjoining bathroom and quickly washed, slipping into the pyjamas with speed.

She slipped between the cool sheets and switched the bedside light off, snuggling down in the comfortable bed with pleasure. She couldn't quite believe that he had really gone to bed, leaving her safe and unharmed. It seemed so out of character with the man she had read about for so long. But people are never what they seem, and Kate wondered exactly what Luke was like, what made him tick, what went on inside that clever black head.

So much had happened that day that she thought she would fall asleep immediately. But her mind refused to close down, and kept skimming over the day's events, running through her day at work, coming home with Linda on the tube, getting changed in a rush for the party which had turned out to be so boring.

Then meeting Luke, driving off in the car with him, talking to him, watching him. She shivered as she recalled the way he had kissed her in the car, her body responding almost as though he was kissing her now. She tried to push away her thoughts, but she found herself reliving again and again his kisses and embraces.

He had aroused in her feelings she had never known existed, and those feelings not only confused her, they opened up a whole new frightening world for her.

CHAPTER TWO

KATE rubbed her eyes wearily. Her limbs felt like lead. It was still quite dark outside. What on earth was that racket going on outside the house? She groaned and turned over in bed, putting the pillow over her head, but the noise continued.

She huddled deeper under the pillow, putting her hands over her ears. Why didn't those people outside shut up? she thought crossly. God, she was tired! Her muscles ached and her throat felt thick from lack of sleep. She opened her eyes tiredly and looked at her watch. Seven o'clock. What did they think they were doing?

She sat up in bed, then flopped back. She was too tired to sit up, let alone go and see what was going on. Perhaps if she wished hard enough, those people would go away. She closed her eyes. Please go away, she thought.

A key turned; the door burst open and Luke came striding in. His face was angry, his eyes narrowed dangerously. Kate pulled the bedclothes up to her chin in the hope that they would protect her.

He glowered down at her, his black brows brooding like menacing thunderclouds.

'Is anything wrong?' she asked brightly.

He threw a newspaper down on her bed and walked over to the light switch. He turned it on, illuminating the bedroom, but making the dark outside seem even darker.

Kate opened the paper slowly, then her mouth dropped open as she read the headlines. LUKE HASTINGS KIDNAPS YOUNG GIRL. She looked at Luke. He was ominously silent.

'Oh dear!' she said.

Luke's teeth snapped together. 'That is an understatement!' he bit out angrily. He came towards her and picked up the paper. 'It was bad enough with the photographs they got last night. But that's nothing compared to the story they've got here.'

'But how did they know?' she asked, sitting up in bed.

'Your bloody friend told them, that's how they know!' he shouted, throwing the paper back at her.

Kate ducked out of its way as it sailed past her head.

'Well, that's not my fault, you don't have to swear at me,' she retorted indignantly.

Luke ignored her, going over to the window instead. He opened it angrily.

'Clear off!' he barked, slamming the window shut again.

Kate sat bolt upright. 'Are they reporters?' she asked.

'That's one name for them,' he snapped.

Kate swallowed and picked up the paper from the floor. She looked at the photographs. There was one of her lying in Luke's arms, her leg twisted in an ungainly fashion beneath her. She wrinkled her nose at it. She looked awful!

There was a smaller photograph of Linda looking

worried, and Kate's eyes flickered over the story. A name jumped out of the page at her: Brian. Oh, God, she thought dismally, Brian knows. But all it said in the paper was ... 'Her boy-friend, Brian Richards, is extremely worried for her safety.' Well, that didn't tell her much.

She chewed her lower lip anxiously as she read the rest of the story, and pulled a face as she saw what she had been dreading. Linda had telephoned her family in the early house of the morning to tell them what had happened and to see if Kate was there. She sighed. Goodness only knew what her parents were thinking. Her father would probably drag her home, labelling her 'unable to take care of herself'.

She frowned. Linda had a lot to explain. Who else had she phoned to let in on the big secret? Practically everyone of importance, it seemed. Well, that was very jolly of Linda. She would have a word with her when she got home!

'What are we going to do?' she asked Luke eventually.

'How the hell do I know?' he yelled.

'Well, we've got to do something,' she pointed out reasonably.

Luke glowered at her menacingly. 'I'm quite well aware of that!' he barked.

Kate made a face. It wasn't her fault any of this had happened. She liked it even less than he did. Besides, it was her reputation that was being busily tarnished, not his.

'The least you can do is be civil about it,' she told him crossly.

His blue eyes narrowed. 'I don't feel very civil at the moment,' he bit out caustically.

Kate compressed her lips. He was worse than Linda! At least when Linda was angry she was quiet about it. Luke exploded all over the place.

'It's no good blaming me,' she said stiffly.

He looked at her impatiently. 'Get out of that bed. You're not going to get any more sleep this morning. You'll be more use to me if you're not lounging around.'

Kate folded her hands calmly and looked him straight in the eye. 'I'll be quite happy to get out of bed and get dressed if you go away,' she told him, remaining where she was.

Luke shot across the room and grabbed her arm, yanking her out of bed before she could stop him, and Kate yelped as she tumbled out of bed, regaining her balance with difficulty.

'When I tell you to get out of bed, I expect you to do it!' he roared, and stormed out of the room, slamming the door behind him.

Kate sighed. Somebody got out of bed the wrong side this morning, she thought crossly. She rubbed her wrist ruefully. Who did he think he was, coming in here shouting and swearing at seven in the morning? He was like a bear with a sore head!

She picked up her clothes and rushed into the bathroom, locking the door behind her. She cleaned her teeth quickly and dragged a brush through her hair. She looked in the mirror. God, she looked awful! She splashed more cold water on her face, trying to put more colour in her cheeks.

It wasn't pleasant, having to put on old clothes,

but she had to put up with it. At least they aren't too creased, she thought glumly, looking down at her dress as she smoothed it over her hips.

She took one last look in the mirror. Oh well, she thought, there's not much salvage work I can do on that face. I'll just have to look pale and interesting.

She mentally chided herself for trying to look as nice as possible. What did she care how she looked? Luke probably wouldn't even notice anyway.

As she came out of the bathroom Luke barked up the stairs, 'What the hell are you doing?'

'I'm coming!' she yelled back hurriedly, scampering down the stairs and into the kitchen from where his voice was coming.

'Well, get a move on!' he shouted back.

He was dressed in a superbly cut black suit, the white silk collar of his shirt open at the neck, exposing the tanned column of his throat. The smooth material of the jacket emphasised the breadth of his powerful shoulders, the trousers of his suit showing to perfection his long, long legs, Kate felt a strange sense of longing, but fought it back, averting her eyes hastily from his muscular thighs.

He looked her over with angry blue eyes, his face set angrily. 'You look like a ghost,' he said abruptly, and turned back to stand by the coffee percolator.

Charming! she thought drily. So much for being pale and interesting. He took two mugs out of one of the wall cupboards, looking across at her briefly as he did so.

'Coffee?' he asked in a clipped voice.

Kate compressed her lips. He wasn't trying to be cheerful. 'Yes, please,' she said politely. If he wanted to rant and rave all morning, that was entirely up to him. She needed to relax. She still felt very tired physically, although she was wide awake mentally. Her arms felt like chewed-up string, and her legs didn't feel much better.

Luke poured the coffee into the two mugs and handed her one of them. He sat down on one of the chairs around the kitchen table, and gestured for her to sit on one too. Kate pulled up another chair, setting her coffee down on the table and sitting down.

The noise outside the house was still very loud. It appeared to have intensified since she had got up. Perhaps more reporters had arrived. She sighed and looked at Luke. He was staring at his coffee, his brows linked in a frown.

Kate cleared her throat. 'Had any ideas?' she asked brightly.

He looked up, his eyes narrowing slightly between thick, sooty lashes. 'What?' he snapped.

'I said, have you had any ideas? About what we're going to do?' she repeated.

He shook his head. 'No,' he said, 'and I don't see that there are many easy ways out of this.'

She sighed. If he wanted to be pessimistic, she couldn't talk him out of it. Miserable pig! she thought with a grimace. She sipped her coffee, her mind busily trying to make some sort of shape out of the tangled mess she was in. There had to be a way out, she thought logically.

Luke muttered something unintelligible, and Kate looked up, startled out of her thoughts by his deep voice.

'What did you say?' she asked in a puzzled voice.

'I'm going to kill that girl when I get my hands on her,' he replied angrily.

Kate frowned. 'What girl?' she asked, puzzled even more.

His eyes shot angry blue sparks at her. 'Your friend Linda!' he shouted. 'I'm going to put her head in a gas oven!'

Kate smothered a chuckle. 'You don't really mean it,' she said, adding hopefully, 'Do you?'

'Try me,' he growled, his face threatening.

Kate swallowed nervously. It appeared that the less said about Linda, the better. Luke would only start blowing up all over the place again. She lapsed into silence, sipping her coffee, a thoughtful frown on her face.

Surely nobody would actually believe that Luke had really kidnapped her? she thought. It was too ludicrous to be true, after all. Anyone with an ounce of common sense would see the story for what it was—a piece of over-exaggerated rubbish by a highly imaginative reporter with an eye to the main chance.

But how many times had she herself wondered at the truth behind the headlines? Rarely, if ever, she conceded dismally. It tended to go into one ear and out of the other without a second thought. She didn't pay much attention to the scandal stories. They always turned out to be nine-day wonders. Apart from that, the lives of the famous and infamous didn't interest her very much.

But what would her family think? They would no doubt believe some grain of truth to be in the story. Of course, she thought wryly, there *was* a certain amount of truth there. But it certainly wasn't a kidnapping, and she was none the worse off for all that had happened the previous night. Luke had made no more advances to her since her stiff rejection of him in the car.

She chewed her lower lip thoughtfully. How were her family and friends supposed to know that? And would they believe her if she told them? Brian would no doubt assume the worst. He was generally very kind and thoughtful towards her. He obviously felt something for her, although she wasn't quite sure how serious he was. She certainly liked him, but she knew he wasn't the man she would marry. Unfortunately he was very suspicious, he was likely to believe the nasty implications of the previous night. She would just have to make him believe her.

Luke suddenly stood up, setting his cup on the table with a distinct crash. He looked down at her broodingly, his face dark and still very angry.

'Come on,' he snapped, 'get your things together, we're going out.'

Kate gulped the rest of her coffee down hastily, picking her handbag up from the floor. 'Where are we going?' she asked as she stood up.

'Visiting,' came the curt reply.

She eyed him suspiciously. 'Visiting who?'

'Your friend Linda,' he told her abruptly, turning and walking out into the hall.

Kate hurried after him. 'You're not going to be nasty to her, are you?' she asked hopefully.

'No, I'll just nail her head to the floor,' he said over his shoulder as they neared the front door.

Kate swallowed nervously. 'She was probably very

worried, Luke,' she said, stopping as she reached the front door where he stood. She didn't know why she was defending Linda after the stupid way she had behaved, but she didn't want Luke to be too nasty to her. He had already shown her how his temper could explode this morning, and she didn't want Linda exposed to that.

He looked at her angrily, his mouth compressed tautly. 'I don't give a damn how worried she was!'

Kate frowned worriedly. 'But shouting at her isn't going to do either of us any good.'

He raked a hand roughly through his thick black hair. His jaw had a determined thrust to it, his mouth compressed in a hard line, his skin taut across his harsh cheekbones. A muscle was going in his cheek as he studied her broodingly.

'You don't seem to give a damn about all that's happened, do you?' he said in a harsh voice with a slight edge to it.

She sighed. 'Of course I do. I just don't see that shouting and bellowing at people is going to get me any farther.'

His eyes narrowed speculatively, a dangerous glint within their depths. 'In fact, I'm beginning to wonder if all this wasn't planned.'

Kate stared at him for a moment. He couldn't be serious! It was just his anger getting the better of him. He couldn't honestly believe that she would plan something like this.

'Don't be absurd,' she told him, her voice slightly nervous as she tried to assess whether or not he was serious.

His face was harsh, his eyes flickering with sparks

of barely controlled anger. He watched her steadily. 'Let me warn you, Kate,' he said grimly, 'it would be a mistake for you to try to make me look a fool.'

She was appalled. How dared he suggest such a thing? She smiled sweetly. 'That wouldn't be too difficult,' she told him with acid injected into her voice. 'But you don't really need my help, you're doing fine all by yourself.'

Luke's mouth compressed into a firm, hard line. Then he moved fast. He took hold of her upper arms in his grip, his fingers pressing into her soft flesh as he held her.

'You're playing a dangerous game, Kate,' he said tightly, his eyes glittering.

She glared at him. 'I am not playing games,' she said, her words separated jerkily by the control she was exerting over her anger.

His eyes narrowed, and his grip tightened on her arms, making her wince as his fingers bit into her flesh. 'If I find out you're behind all this, I'll make you pay hell for it,' he said harshly.

Kate pushed at his powerful chest, trying to wriggle out of his grasp. He held her still, exerting more strength.

'Let me go!' she snapped.

'I despise cheats,' Luke said coldly, ignoring her struggles.

Kate stood still, giving up the idea of getting out of his grip. He looked extremely dangerous, his face grim and forbidding. She looked up at him once more. 'I've had nothing whatsoever to do with any of this,' she told him angrily, 'and I don't see why you should think I have.'

Luke studied her. 'You have a talent for acting,' he said with an edge to his voice.

'And you have a very fertile imagination,' she snapped, resuming her struggles with fervour. How dared he suggest that she had had anything to do with this? As far as she could see, he was merely looking for someone on whom he could lay the blame.

The doorbell stopped her struggles. They both turned to look at the front door, then Luke released her slowly. 'Who the hell is that?' he murmured as he moved to the door.

Kate rubbed her arms resentfully, standing back as he opened the door. Great crowds of people pushed forward, their faces eager. They shouted questions at him, flashbulbs going off at all angles. They looked like a swarm of bees in search of honey as they moved as one body towards Luke.

She stepped back instinctively, horrified at the number of people she saw. Then she saw the woman. Luke grabbed her arm and pulled her inside the door, slamming it behind them quickly.

Kate recognised her immediately—Lisa Blair, Luke's agent for the past four years. She stood in the hallway, smiling at Luke, her long blonde hair flowing in waves down her slender back. Her eyes were dark, small slits in her sun-tanned face. Her skin was the colour of honey, golden-brown, her cheekbones high, skilfully defined with blusher. Her lips glistened with lip-gloss, her teeth were small and white. Lisa Blair was the ultimate picture of elegant chic. Her early training in modelling had stayed ingrained in her, even though she had given up her career in favour of becoming an agent to the rich and famous.

'Darling, I came as soon as I could,' she murmured in a voice like honey, smiling up at him.

Luke leaned forward and placed a kiss on her cheek. 'I could do with some help,' he said, a slight smile curving his hard mouth.

Lisa laughed throatily. 'When have I ever let you down?' she asked rhetorically, and Luke smiled slightly, his blue eyes flickering over her. Lisa paused fractionally, her eyes darting towards Kate, narrowed slightly, making them appear even smaller. 'It isn't true of course, is it?' she asked hesitantly, her small white teeth slightly exposed as she watched Luke intently.

He shook his head. 'You know better than to ask that, Lisa,' he told her, his eyes glittering with something resembling amusement.

Kate imagined that Lisa wasn't sure she did know better than that. She looked at the elegant woman standing next to Luke, taking in the almost imperceptible flicker of relief in her small brown eyes. She wondered if Lisa was in love with Luke. It had been rumoured in the papers that there had been an affair between them, but Kate knew now how the papers could twist things out of proportion.

Lisa looked over at Kate. 'She looks awfully pale, Luke,' she said, laughing nervously. 'What have you been doing to her?' Again she watched Luke intently as she spoke, although her voice was deliberately casual.

Luke looked at Kate, his electric blue eyes flickering over her slowly, his mouth taking on a grim line once more. 'Nothing,' he said in a cold voice.

Lisa smiled. 'Well, that certainly makes my job easier,' she said. 'Now all I have to do is get the general public to believe it.'

Luke smiled without humour. 'I think that's highly unlikely. People tend to believe only what they want to believe. You're going to have a difficult job unless we think of some other way out of it.'

Lisa shrugged elegantly, sliding her hands into the pockets of her exquisitely cut grey trousers. 'In that case, we'll just have to think of another way out of it.'

She looks as if she has stepped straight out of the pages of *Harpers and Queen*, Kate thought ruefully. Her red silk shirt hung elegantly on her fine-boned body, contrasting beautifully with the grey French-cut trousers, her tiny waist emphasised by a slim leather belt. She wore three very long gold chains casually around her neck, falling to her waist, completing the picture of understated opulence.

Luke moved towards Lisa, smiling down at her. 'Shall we go into the lounge to discuss this?' he said casually.

Lisa nodded and opened the door on her right, moving into the room as though she had lived in the house all her life. Luke followed her slowly. Kate didn't know quite what to do. She wasn't sure if the invitation had been extended to her or not. She decided it would be better to stay where she was and wait to see if Luke asked her in.

He turned as he went into the room, his face expressionless as he looked at her. 'You'd better come in too,' he said coldly.

Kate stiffened at his tone. Her lips tightened

angrily, but she made no reply, merely followed him in with her chin lifted slightly.

The room was very large and tastefully furnished, giving the appearance of warmth and comfort. She had a feeling that some of the pieces of furniture were antique, the rich glow of the wood was evidently very expensive.

Lisa was reclining gracefully in a large, comfortable-looking armchair, her long, slim hands curling on the arm of the chair. Kate sat in the chair opposite, her hands held stiffly in her lap, her back straight, while Luke sat down on the settee, his long legs stretched lazily in front of him.

Lisa smiled at Luke. 'I think it would make life a lot easier if you could fill in the details for me. After all, I only know what I've read in the papers.'

Luke watched her steadily, his blue eyes enigmatic. 'What do you want to know?' he asked lazily.

Lisa shrugged, her small brown eyes darting across to Kate, then back to Luke. 'Anything that you think might be relevant,' she said, a little too casually.

Kate watched Luke. He seemed totally at ease with Lisa. How well did he know her? she wondered. Was she just his agent, a business associate as well as a friend, or was she something more? She found herself wondering if Lisa had in fact been his mistress at one time. Looking at the woman in question, Kate felt a sharp sensation in the pit of her stomach, but she hurriedly pushed away the feeling, turning her eyes back to Luke.

He leaned back in the settee, a grim smile etched on his face. 'I don't really think any of it is relevant. What happened last night was wildly over-exaggerated by the newspapers. Anything we tell them concerning last night is certain to be misconstrued. It would be better if we could find a valid reason for what happened.'

Lisa's eyes narrowed slightly, and she leaned forward in her chair. 'That's true enough,' she said, 'but I feel I must have some idea of what actually did happen, rather than just make wild guesses.'

Kate noticed the sudden tension reappear in Lisa's body as she spoke to Luke. 'Nothing happened last night,' she interrupted quickly, and Luke and Lisa both looked at her in surprise. 'I hurt my ankle and Luke put me in the car, that's all,' she finished.

Lisa looked at her questioningly, her eyes narrowing into tiny slits in her face. 'If that's all that happened, how did you end up staying here all night?' she asked, making her voice appear casual, but it had a slight edge to it as her eyes pinned Kate down.

Kate shrugged. 'I didn't have my keys with me. I was locked out of my flat, so Luke very kindly offered to put me up for the night,' she said, throwing him an icy look.

'Is that true?' Lisa asked him.

He nodded. 'That's exactly what happened,' he told her calmly. 'I can't imagine why anyone should think I would want to kidnap someone. They're just after a sensation.'

Lisa laughed. She then launched into a number of ideas she had had while driving over to the house that morning. Most of them were rejected firmly by Luke, with one or two discussed thoroughly and then rejected. Kate lapsed into a steady silence, listening with one ear, but not really taking much in.

It seemed to her that all they were concerned about was his reputation, not hers. It angered her at first, but after a while she recognised that much of what he said concerned both of them. He was rejecting a lot of ideas on the basis that nobody would believe them, and it would only cause further damage to Kate as well as to him.

Kate wondered why all this had happened to her. After all, it was such an unlikely situation to be in that it was rather like being dropped into a comedy of errors. One thing after another had gone wrong for her, starting the minute she had laid eyes on Luke last night.

'Well?' Luke's deep voice brought her out of her thoughts.

She looked up startled, her eyes questioning. 'I'm sorry, I wasn't listening,' she said.

Luke sighed. He raked a hand through his hair, his eyes hooded, looking at her between thick black lashes. 'I wish you'd keep your mind on what we're saying,' he said. 'It would make things a lot easier.'

Kate blushed slightly, feeling Lisa's derisive eyes fixed upon her. 'Sorry,' she mumbled. 'What were you saying?'

'The only possible solution we've come up with so far is this: If we tell them that you are in fact a relative of mine, and that you were visiting me, it might just work. It's the only plausible explanation,' he told her calmly.

Kate frowned. 'I don't see why we can't tell them what really happened. Surely they'd realise that everyone makes mistakes at some time or another?'

Luke's eyes narrowed, his mouth compressing into a hard line. 'Are you trying to be obstructive?' he questioned harshly.

'No,' she said defensively, looking at Lisa out of the corner of her eye, 'I just thought it might be better. They must know that it wasn't what they've reported it to be.'

Luke's teeth snapped together with exasperation. 'That has nothing whatsoever to do with it,' he said angrily. 'Whether or not they believe what they've written is irrelevant. The implications are there and we've got to act quickly if we're to salvage our reputations. I would have thought that you would be worried enough about your good name to want to find a solution instead of sitting there staring into space and making absurd remarks.'

Kate's eyebrows rose. 'There's no need to be quite so nasty about it,' she said reasonably.

'There is every need!' Luke said angrily. 'We only have a limited amount of time in which to make an announcement, so we have to act fast. I need your co-operation on this. I can't go out there and tell them you're my cousin if you step out and deny it.'

Kate swallowed nervously at the tone of his voice. She glanced at Lisa, who was relaxing in her chair with a slight smile on her face. She's enjoying this, Kate thought crossly.

'Very well,' she shrugged. 'If you think it's the only solution, go and make the announcement. But I still don't think they're going to believe it.'

Luke gave her a look which made her want to crawl into a large black hole. 'You'll have to make them believe it,' he said icily.

Kate shivered. His eyes were like brilliant chips of ice as he looked at her, his face harsh and controlled. He stood up, uncoiling his long legs with a fluid graceful movement.

'Lisa,' he said, turning to her, 'go and make the announcement and tell them we'll be out in a short while to confirm it. Anything they want to ask can be directed to my offices. And tell them to get the hell off my property. If they want to wait, they can wait in the street, not my front garden.'

Lisa stood up elegantly, smiling. 'Okay. I shan't be long.' And she went out of the room, moving her long slim body seductively.

Luke looked down at Kate. 'I'll make some more coffee. Come in the kitchen and I'll explain exactly what you'll have to do.' He walked out of the room briskly without a backward glance.

Kate got up and followed his crossly. He had been deliberately rude to her in front of Lisa. It had been very embarrassing for her, and Lisa had sat and watched like a Cheshire Cat, with an almost smug smile on her beautifully painted face.

Luke switched on the hotplate beneath the coffee pot. He motioned for her to sit down and turned back to making the coffee, and Kate sat down, leaning her chin in her hands. She was positive that whatever they told the press would be dismissed as being a fabrication. If that was the case, why not just tell them the truth and have done with it?

'Snap out of it!' Luke commanded harshly, glaring at her as she sat up instantly.

'Now what have I done?' she asked defensively.

'You were daydreaming again,' he told her, taking

three cups out of the cupboard. He turned back to her, leaning against one of the kitchen surfaces, his arms folded across his powerful chest.

'I wasn't,' she protested. 'I was just thinking.'

He raised one jet-black brow. 'It amounts to the same thing, I believe,' he told her without humour. He slid his hands into his pockets, standing with legs apart. 'I'll tell you everything you're going to have to do, if you're ready to listen.'

She blushed slightly. 'Of course I'm listening!'

He watched her steadily, the blue eyes enigmatic. 'Right, if you're my cousin, that makes your parents my relatives too. Which in turn makes things rather difficult if your parents refuse to go along with the story. Unfortunately, they've already been contacted about this, so it will have to have been a recent discovery. Therefore I'll drive you down to your family and explain the situation, and hope they agree to support our story.'

Kate frowned. 'First of all you'll have to get them to believe that nothing actually happened between us,' she said, beginning to flush slightly as she finished the sentence.

He smiled grimly. 'I'm aware of that. Which is why we'll be driving down to see them as soon as possible.'

Kate sighed. She wasn't sure he was going to have an easy job on his hands. But what good would it do to tell him that? She made a face. He would only get angry with her again, and that made her very jumpy and nervous.

'May I make a suggestion?' she ventured.

His brows rose slightly. 'By all means.'

Kate cleared her throat, picking her words carefully before she actually spoke. She didn't want him jumping down her throat over the least thing. 'Well, I think perhaps it would be better if you told them I was your second cousin, rather than an immediate relative. It won't be so hard to get out of at a later date. Apart from that,' she paused, making sure he was listening, 'it won't be as easy to disprove, should anyone decide to try.'

Luke didn't speak when she had finished. He stood watching her, his blue eyes hooded, his face unreadable, while Kate watched him, avoiding his eyes as carefully as she could. The silence lengthened. She swallowed nervously, feeling a little frightened by his stillness. He looked like a sleek panther closing in for the kill, poised ready to leap on his victim.

'That's my suggestion,' she said stupidly, feeling the need to break the ominous silence that had developed between them. She eyed him warily, wishing he would speak, but he merely continued watching her, with a glint in his eye that she didn't quite like. 'Well?' she prompted, tension seeping into her.

Luke leaned forward, placing his hands on the table in front of her. His head was close to hers as she looked up into his deep blue eyes, his face inches from her own. At such close quarters, she could see the control he was exerting over his temper, a muscle jerking in his cheek as he bent close to her.

'You haven't listened to a word I've said,' he said between clenched teeth. 'All the time we were talking in the lounge, and all that I've said to you has gone in one ear and straight out of the other.'

She backed her head away slightly, frightened by

the close proximity. 'What do you mean?' she faltered.

'You know damn well what I mean,' he bit out. 'The suggestion you just made is the very one I posed to you at least ten minutes ago in the lounge.'

Kate blushed. 'Well, I didn't know,' she mumbled.

'I think you did,' he told her harshly. 'In fact, I've got the idea that you're just trying to waste time. Or perhaps you don't like the way this has turned out.'

She stared at him. What was he accusing her of now? she wondered as surprise mingled with realisation. 'Are you saying that you still believe I was responsible for all this?' she asked incredulously.

He moved closer. 'That is exactly what I'm saying. What did you expect to happen, I wonder? Did you think I would try to cover this mess by becoming your lover? Getting engaged to you, perhaps? Is that why you held me off last night? To add a little mystery to your attractions?'

She gasped, startled into anger by his vile accusations. 'How dare you!' she snapped angrily. 'Only someone with a disgusting mind could dream up something as vile as what you're suggesting! Which is why you're suggesting it—because you have a mind like a sewer!'

Luke smiled grimly. 'I think the insults are directed at the wrong person.'

Her lips tightened into a thin, angry line. 'You're beginning to believe your own publicity,' she snapped.

He tilted his black head to one side, watching her

steadily with blue eyes which glittered dangerously as he spoke so softly that at first she thought she hadn't heard him. 'Meaning?' he queried.

'Meaning,' she said in an equally quiet voice, 'that you are beginning to believe that you're irresistible.'

His eyes narrowed dangerously, his face tightening as he held on to his temper. 'Little girls who play with fire must expect to get burned.'

'Stop speaking in riddles!' she snapped. 'You've had more to do with this mess than I have, and I'm not interested in your ridiculous accusations. You're just looking around for someone you can lay the blame on.'

She stood up and turned her back on him, beginning to walk out of the kitchen. Her back was rigid with indignation and anger, and she could feel her blood boiling with the desire to hit out at him for all the vile things he had said to her.

'Not so fast!' Luke ground out, taking hold of her and swinging her round to face him, his eyes blazingly angry as she stared up into them. 'Where the hell do you think you're going?'

'I'm going home,' she snapped. 'I don't see that anything you say or do is going to make any difference to what people believe or think. They will believe, as you so rightly said before, exactly what they want to believe. If that's the case, I don't see why I shouldn't go home and try to live it down.'

'Don't be so stupid!' Luke snarled. He pulled her shoulders towards him, his hand moving quickly to press into the small of her back, until she was against him. Kate struggled, staring up at him with wide, frightened eyes. His face was so close to hers that she could feel his breath on her hair. She smelt the male, very musky scent of his body.

'Let go of me!' she whispered angrily, fear and excitement beginning to rise inside her.

His answer was to grip the back of her neck with his hand, his other hand still pressing her against him as she struggled to be free. 'If you walked out of here alone,' he said through his teeth, 'do you have any idea of what that would make you look like?'

She stopped struggling, pressing her hands flat against his chest. 'Yes,' she said bitterly, 'and I don't care. I'd rather hear their insults than yours!'

His eyes blazed with anger. 'You stubborn little fool,' he bit out, his jaw taut, his teeth clenched. 'You'll damned well stay here and do as you're told!'

'Get lost!' she hissed, meeting his eyes. Their eyes locked, warring silently, each one angry with the other, yet too proud to give in.

Suddenly the atmosphere changed. It was so unexpected that her breath caught in her throat, her heart started to thump heavily, and she stared helplessly into his eyes.

CHAPTER THREE

HE gazed down at her, his eyes beginning to darken as he held her. Kate thought she could feel every muscle in his entire body, each part of her body leaping with flames of awareness as he pressed her against him.

His thighs were hard against her legs, his chest powerful beneath her hands. The hand on her neck began to relax, starting a soothing motion, sending tingles of excitement coursing through her body. His sexuality was suddenly more overwhelming than it had ever been, sending her dizzy with sensations she had no power to control.

They were both for an instant motionless. Silence clung to them as the atmosphere changed.

'God!' Luke murmured under his breath, his voice husky. Then his head moved slowly closer, his eyes open, black with desire, watching her face as he came closer, and closer.

Kate's eyes widened, then she tilted her head back unconsciously, waiting breathlessly to receive his kiss. Her heart pounded against her breastbone, her pulses were ringing in her ears.

His mouth touched hers gently, his lips tantalising her as his hands pressed her softly against him. She melted her body against his, needing to feel as though she was a part of his hard, male body. She didn't realise that by doing so, she inflamed him further.

Luke groaned as he felt the warm, soft female slide submissively into his arms. He increased the pressure on her lips, slowly opening her mouth, his hand caressing her back. She heard herself groan with pleasure, felt herself slide her arms up and around his neck, her fingers tangling in his thick black hair. Her confusion added to the excitement she felt. She had no knowledge of how to react, how to respond.

Her mind whirled until she could no longer make the effort to think. She concentrated instead on the beautiful feelings flooding through her, allowing her body to follow what seemed most natural.

His mouth left hers, blazing a slow, tantalising trail across her cheek to her throat. He dropped light kisses on the sensitive skin of her neck, inducing the most exhilarating tingling sensations that left her breathless.

His strong white teeth nibbled gently against her throat, her heart crashed in her ears, deafening her, while her senses responded wildly to his touch.

His mouth left her neck, and he moved his head up, looking at her with almost black eyes, half closed, fringed with thick black lashes. 'Kate,' he groaned, his mouth brushing hers gently, his hands caressing her back with increasing pressure. 'Oh God, you're intoxicating,' he muttered throatily, almost with a groan of reluctance.

His mouth opened hers, kissing her deeply. His hands moved down to her waist, caressing her slowly, bringing her hands round to her stomach, then slowly he moved his hands upwards, nearer and nearer to her breasts.

Her blood pressure rocketed. She arched against him, needing to be touched by him, senseless, oblivious to everything around her.

'Luke!'

Lisa's voice brought them apart instantly. Kate whirled round to face her. She stood in the doorway with a hand to her mouth, her eyes wide with shock.

Shutters came down on Lisa's face automatically. Luke looked up at her, his face slightly tinged with deep red, his eyes narrowed, his breathing uneven.

Lisa looked from one to the other. Her eyes narrowed until they were merely dark slits in her face, making her look like an Egyptian queen.

'Kissing cousins,' she drawled spitefully, 'Well, well, well!'

It was extremely unwell, Kate thought as her mind began working coherently. After what she must have seen, and Kate knew it couldn't have looked very nice, Lisa must now believe that she had slept with Luke the previous night.

She felt herself colour with a burning red. She looked pleadingly at Luke, hoping he would explain to Lisa that what she had seen had not been what it seemed, but Luke didn't meet her eyes. He was looking over the top of her head at Lisa.

'I'd like a word with you, Lisa,' Luke said in a deep, quiet tone. He released Kate, and she stood back from his immediately, keeping her eyes averted from Lisa's.

Lisa's pretty red lips parted spitefully. 'I'm sure you would,' she drawled, folding her arms and looking him straight in the eye.

Luke moved forward and took her arm, turning

her around and leading her out of the kitchen. He looked back at Kate. 'Make yourself that coffee I promised you,' he said quietly. 'I'll be back in a minute,' and he took Lisa into the lounge, closing the door firmly behind him.

Kate sat down dazedly in a chair. What on earth had happened to her to make her behave like that? Luke Hastings happened to me, she thought grimly. She stared at the floor unseeingly, her mind taking her back to the moment when the atmosphere had so suddenly and confusingly changed between them.

She relived every detail of his embrace, felt once again his lips on hers, his touch on her back and stomach, and a slight smile touched her lips as she felt a small recurrence of the sensations he had aroused in her.

Then she remembered Lisa, standing in the doorway, watching for goodness only knew how long. What had it looked like through Lisa's eyes? Kate crimsoned, putting her hands to her hot cheeks with shame. It could only have looked like exactly what it was; Kate pressing against Luke with abandonment, her arms entwined around his neck, allowing him to kiss her like that.

She had been kissed before, but never like that. Her experience was vastly limited, compared with Luke's obvious familiarity with the senses. He had known exactly how to kiss her, his finger on the pulse spot the whole time. He knew how to operate women. It was as though he had pressed a series of magic buttons on her body, eliciting a response which took her by storm.

Kate felt her heart take a nose-dive as she realised

that her thoughts were correct. He probably only thought of her as another woman, another conquest.

The elation she had felt was replaced with a sense of hopelessness. The beauty and magic inside her collapsed like a balloon, leaving her feeling ashamed and unwanted.

She sighed heavily, getting up to make herself some coffee. She stood by the coffee maker, staring into space with glazed eyes, seeing nothing, lost in her own thoughts.

As she was drinking her coffee, her face distant, her mind confused, she heard the door of the lounge open, then footsteps came towards her as Luke strode into the kitchen.

He looked down at her, his black head tilted to one side, 'Daydreaming again?' he queried.

Kate looked up at him, her eyes wide, green and very confused. 'No, I was just waiting for you,' she told him quietly, hoping he couldn't see through her eyes and into her mind.

Lisa appeared in the doorway, sliding her hands into the pockets of her trousers and leaning elegantly against the door. 'You'd better get ready to face the press,' she said, her lips parting to reveal small white teeth.

Kate looked at her silently. There was an unmistakable air of triumph and superiority about her that jarred on Kate's nerves. What had Luke said to her, she wondered, that could have had such an effect?

'Where are we going?' she asked, looking back at Luke.

His face was unreadable, his blue eyes hooded,

hiding his thoughts from her.

'First,' he said expressionlessly. 'We'll take you back to your flat. I want to find out what your friend told the papers, and if they might be able to use it against us in the next edition. Then we'll drive you down to your parents' house. Where do they live?'

'Essex,' she replied automatically, her voice quiet and uncertain as she continued to wonder what Luke had said to Lisa about her.

'That's not too far,' drawled Lisa, her slim hands fiddling absently with the long gold chains around her neck. 'You'll be back in time for tea, so to speak.'

Luke smiled grimly. 'I think not,' he said in a dark voice. 'Kate's parents are not going to be easily persuaded that their daughter has been safe in my care.'

Lisa shrugged elegantly, the movement rippling the expensive silk of her blouse. 'It shouldn't take you that long,' she said in silky tones.

Luke didn't reply. He turned to Kate. 'Get your things together. We'll leave as soon as you're ready.'

Kate smiled tightly. 'I'm ready now,' she told them, standing up and picking up her handbag as she followed them into the hall. She picked out her coat from the rack.

Luke helped her on with it, his fingers brushing her skin making her jump away from his touch like a scalded cat. He gave her a dry look, and she averted her eyes, waiting while he put his own black cashmere overcoat on.

'Is everyone ready,' he asked, his hand on the door catch. Lisa and Kate nodded, and Luke said, 'This

isn't going to be easy. Kate, I want you to stay close
to me, don't answer any questions unless I tell you
to. Just walk to the car and cling on to me.' He
watched her briefly as she nodded in acknowledge-
ment. 'Lisa,' he continued, 'you know what to do, so
just make sure nobody corners Kate. You'd better
follow in your car, it'll make it easier when I have to
take Kate to her parents' house.'

Lisa looked sulky for a moment, but finally
nodded. 'Okay, I'm ready.'

Luke looked at both of them. 'Here we go, then,'
he said, and opened the door.

Kate stepped back instinctively as the men and
women pushed forwards, and flashbulbs went off in
all directions, blinding her as Luke pulled her out of
the house.

His hand was clamped firmly around her wrist as
he walked quickly, pushing his way through the reporters who barraged them both with questions.
Luke shouted replies to a few questions, mainly
stating that he was going to see his newly-dis-
covered cousin's family. Kate shrank with horror
as she saw the knowing, leering faces grinning at
her.

One of the men shouted a question Which, even to
Kate's ears, sounded obscene in its implications.
Some of the reporters laughed at the double enten-
dre, leering at her as they did so, and Luke threw
them a glacial look, his eyes chips of ice as he carried
on walking.

The car door was opened, and Luke pushed her
inside, slamming the door and walking round to the
other side of the car. He slid in the driving seat,

closing his door to shut out the terrible noise of the reporters.

As he started the car, the men and women outside it circled around them like buzzards. Kate turned her head away as a face pushed up against the glass window next to her.

Luke drove through them, ignoring their cries of disappointment, and soon they were on the main road.

Kate turned to look at Luke as he drove. His profile was harsh, and she wondered if he was still angry. She cleared her throat.

'That was frightening,' she said quietly into the silence that had developed between them.

Luke glanced across at her, his blue eyes impassive. He wasn't angry, merely irritated, that was obvious. 'You're going to have to face them again. They're bound to have your flat staked out, although I doubt if your parents' house will be covered.'

Kate swallowed. She didn't particularly want to have to go through that again. The memory of those leering faces pushing up towards her was still fresh in her mind.

'Is your life always so hectic?' she asked nervously, looking at him through her lashes.

A slight smile touched the corners of his hard mouth. 'Only since I met you,' he said drily.

Kate smiled. She didn't believe that for a second. His life must be a continual irritation, with all the pressmen and photographers permanently on his tail. Kate wondered how he had cultivated his patience. She knew she would become very angry indeed if her privacy was continually invaded like this.

They turned into the road where her flat was. As

Luke had predicted, there were people teeming all around her flat, cameras at the ready as they waited for Kate's arrival.

Luke leaned over as the reporters spotted the car. 'I'll come round and let you out,' he told her as they pulled up outside the flat. 'Just sit tight and wait.'

He got out of the car and forced his way through to her side. Kate marvelled at him—he took it all in his stride. He opened her door, taking hold of her wrist firmly, and pulling her through the crowd. Flashbulbs went off in her face, questions were shouted as Luke began to move towards the front door.

She saw Lisa battling her way through to them, and stifled a grin as she saw a female reporter elbow her in the nose. Lisa caught up with them at the front door, her face flushed and irritated.

'It's not so bad at this end,' she observed, 'but it's bad enough. They look like a collection of starving buzzards!'

Luke raised one eybrow as he pressed the doorbell calmly. 'If it weren't for the starving buzzards, you'd be out of a job,' he told her with wry amusement.

Kate listened to this exchange with a nonchalant expression. It didn't seem as though they were lovers—they certainly didn't talk to each other as though they were. But he was used to covering his private life beneath the shelter of lies. Was that what he was doing with Lisa?

Footsteps bounded down the stairs, and the door was opened. Linda's bubbly blonde head appeared. 'Kate!' she shrieked, flinging the door open to allow them all to step in. 'Where on earth have you been?

I've been worried sick all night!'

Luke closed the door firmly behind them, closing out a major portion of the noise.

Kate eyed Linda wryly. 'Oh, I was fine until I read the papers this morning,' she said, knowing that Linda wouldn't understand the little dig.

Linda smiled vacantly. Then she noticed Luke, and her large blue eyes threatened to engulf the rest of her face. 'You!' she hissed dramatically. 'What are you doing here?'

'I came to see you.' Luke's eyebrows rose slightly as he took in her accusing look.

Linda's mouth formed a large 'O'. 'Me?' she squeaked. 'What on earth for?'

'Let's just say,' said Luke, shooting Kate an amused glance, 'that I want to have a word with you about something.'

Linda shook her head vaguely, then turned back to Kate. 'I thought you'd been murdered and bundled into a locker at Victoria Station,' she informed her with great import.

Kate smiled. 'Really?' This girl, she thought, is an idiot. I've been living with an idiot. She took Linda's arm and led her upstairs. 'Come on, we'd better go upstairs and have some coffee.'

They all went up into the first floor flat. Luke closed the door and turned to Kate. 'You'd better make the coffee while I talk to Linda.'

Kate sighed. There was little she could do to save the poor girl from Luke's irritation. 'Okay,' she said with a shrug.

Linda turned round at that moment, and said in a hushed voice, 'Oh, Kate, I forgot to tell you.' Her voice lowered to a confiding whisper. 'Brian's here.'

Kate's heart sank into her boots. 'What's he doing here?'

Linda looked surprised. 'I thought you'd want to see him. He's been here since seven this morning. Poor Brian, he was terribly worried about you.'

'Poor Brian indeed,' Kate muttered viciously. She didn't think she could face him at the moment.

Luke had obviously been listening. He looked down at her frowning face, raising an eyebrow with amusement as he did so. 'Who's Brian? Your boyfriend?'

Kate nodded glumly. 'Yes, and I don't know what on earth I'm going to say to him.'

Luke laughed. 'Better think up something quickly. He's not likely to believe we're cousins.'

Kate glared at him. After the fuss he'd made about making people believe the story, he might have had the decency not to make a remark like that! She smiled sweetly at him. 'That's not my problem,' she told him. 'He's a six-foot-eight boxer.'

Luke half-smiled, not quite sure how to take that remark. Kate chuckled to herself.

They all went into the living room, Kate first, her eyes averted from the man sitting on the sofa. As she entered the room, Brian stood up, putting a cup down on the table and coming towards her.

'Kate!' he exclaimed, staring at her. His mousey blond hair fell over his forehead, and he pushed it back with a well-manicured hand. His brown eyes were wide and enquiring, set in a slightly pallid face, although the pallor wasn't due to worry—he always looked like that.

'Hello, Brian,' Kate said glumly.

He stretched out his arms in a dramatic gesture and took her in his arms, squeezing her gently. He kissed the top of her head. 'I was so worried,' he whispered against her hair, but when he pulled away to look at her, she didn't notice a sign of worry in the smooth, bland face.

Kate smiled. 'I'm okay,' she told him, her eyes searching his clear brown eyes for a sign of anxiety. But it was useless. He obviously found the whole wretched situation more exciting than worrying.

Her green eyes scanned the flat, as though seeing it from outside herself. It all looked so different, so strange, almost as though she had never lived here before. So much had happened in the last twenty-four hours that it was going to be difficult to resume her old way of life. Even Linda seemed far behind her now. Kate felt sad, suddenly, detached from her friend and her home.

Brian lifted his head from her shoulder. 'What happened?' he asked, giving Luke a hard stare. 'Where did you go?'

'She was in good hands,' Lisa drawled spitefully, her slanted eyes laughing at Kate.

Brian looked round at Lisa, his eyes widening as they ran over her, seeing only the beautiful face and sensual figure, missing the mocking laughter in her eyes.

'Who are you?' Brian was obviously impressed.

'I'm Lisa Blair,' came the husky reply, 'Luke's agent,' and she flashed her pretty white teeth at him.

Brian smiled back at her, and Kate wondered

what she had ever seen in him. He only saw surface
qualities—he was not the man she had first thought
him to be. He hadn't been worried about Kate at
all, that much was evident.

'I'm Brian,' he said, walking towards Lisa, and
taking her hand in a flirtatious handshake, 'Kate's
boy-friend.'

Kate crimsoned, seeing the way his eyes smiled
down at Lisa. She was angry with herself for accept-
ing Brian's invitations to go out in the first place.
She had only done so because she had thought he
was genuine. He had been so persistent; following
her around for a while before she actually agreed to
see him. Then he had insisted on seeing her practically every night, wining and dining her in style,
when she would have been quite happy to spend an
evening at the cinema.

She looked at Luke, who was watching Lisa and
Brian with a wry smile on his face. He caught Kate's
eye, and tilted his head to one side. Kate understood
the gesture. He was saying: 'What did you expect?'

It was Luke who broke into their animated conversation. 'Lisa,' he said in a deep voice, 'I think
we'd better talk to Linda now. We don't have much
time.'

Lisa smiled. 'Of course, darling,' she purred, looking at Kate. 'If you'll excuse us . . .?'

Kate nodded stiffly. 'Of course. I'll go and make
some coffee.' She glanced at Linda, who smiled back
at her, her eyes as trusting and happy as a puppy
dog's, and Kate bit her lip. She hoped Luke wouldn't
be too hard on her.

'I'll help you make the coffee,' Brian said, walking

over to her, and throwing a backward smile at Lisa.

Kate sighed. Brian was very quickly falling in her esteem. She closed the door behind them and walked silently into the kitchen.

He sat down on the stool while she made the coffee. She deliberately kept silent in the hope that Brian wouldn't ask any questions—but it was too much to hope for.

'Come on, then,' Brian asked cheerfully, 'what happened?'

Kate stared at him in amazement. He wasn't reacting the way he should have been. His girl-friend had been supposedly kidnapped by a wealthy, very famous man who had a reputation like fire to boot. Why didn't he react the way he should?

'Nothing happened,' she said in a flat voice.

He laughed. 'Don't be silly! Something must have happened. Tell me.'

Her lips tightened. She was angry with herself for not recognising his shallow nature beforehand. He had hidden his true character well enough for her not to see it clearly.

Or was it, a little voice asked her, that her meeting Luke had made her lose interest? She pushed the thought away hurriedly. But she couldn't deny the fact that, beside Luke, Brian was a lot less interesting.

She sighed, spooning coffee into the mugs. 'Look, Brian, all that happened was that I got locked out all night, and Luke offered to put me up for the night.'

He smiled disbelievingly. 'What else happened?'

Kate put down the spoon with a distinct crash. 'Nothing!'

Brian stood up, grinning. 'Come on, Kate, I know better than that.'

She looked at him with open eyes, seeing the charming character he had built up for her benefit falling away before her eyes.

'I don't think you do,' she said sadly. She had liked Brian before today. She had thought he was a kind, understanding man. The fact that he was good-looking had been a bonus, but she had thought she liked his character. Now, the veil was stripped away, leaving only a shallow youth.

'Now listen,' Brian's eyes narrowed, 'I'm not going to believe that you spent the night with Luke Hastings and absolutely nothing happened. If you thought I would, then you're a fool.'

She shook her head. 'You're quite right, I didn't expect you to believe it. But I *am* telling you the truth. Absolutely nothing happened between us last night.'

Brian made a derisive sound and his face took on a sarcastic expression. 'I suppose you want me to believe he didn't even kiss you?'

Kate felt herself blush as she remembered Luke kissing her in the kitchen. She avoided Brian's eyes.

'I thought so,' said Brian, 'What else did he do?'

'Brian, I've told you—absolutely nothing. Now it's up to you whether you believe me or not. All I can do is tell you the truth—the rest is up to you.'

He laughed harshly. 'That's right, it's up to me. And I don't believe a word of it. If he had you in his house for the night, and he kissed you at one stage, then he must have taken you to bed with him.'

Her lips tightened with anger. She had known it would be difficult, but not this bad. It was amazing how the smooth façade had cracked wide open to show her how unsuitable he really was.

'Well, he didn't. Because I didn't want him to. He did kiss me, yes, but that's all. I stopped him kissing me, and I made it obvious that I didn't want him to try again. Being a gentleman, he left it at that,' she said, her eyes sparking angrily.

'Well, I don't buy it, lady,' Brian said nastily.

Kate shrugged. 'That's your business. Quite frankly, I don't give a damn.'

He took hold of her arms, turning her to face him. 'You don't get rid of me that easily, so you needn't think you will.'

'I wouldn't dream of it,' she said sweetly, giving him a blistering smile. 'It's obviously going to take a lot more than that to get rid of you.'

His eyes narrowed. 'You little bitch! You'll be sorry you said that.'

'I'm sorry I ever met you,' she told him calmly. 'I think you'd better go.'

He shook his head, his eyes angry. He had the look of a little boy being denied the pleasure of something he wanted. His ego had been dented by what she had said, and that was obviously the one thing that would infuriate him above all else.

'I've seen you practically every night for a fortnight,' he said nastily, 'and every time I've come within touching distance, you've slapped my hand down. Why should I stand back and watch you fall into Hastings' bed like a ripe plum?'

Kate realised what he had been up to. He had

thought he would eventually charm her into bed if he kept up the act long enough. She was sickened. She wouldn't have given in even if he had spent ten years trying to seduce her.

She looked at him with disgust. 'Get out!'

His eyes flashed petulantly, then he grabbed her by the waist and slammed her up against the wall, pressing his mouth on hers. Kate pushed at his chest, her hands balled into fists, staring at him with wide, frightened eyes. She should have realised what would happen. How could she be so blind?

She twisted her head away, trying to escape his kisses. As her mouth moved away from his, she screamed, her voice throbbing with sick panic, but Brian pulled her back with a rough jerk, clamping his mouth against hers.

She squirmed with disgust as his hands roved over her body, touching her, squeezing her. She started hitting out at him, pushing, slapping his hands away from her.

'Get your damned hands off her!' Luke's icy voice sliced across the room like a whip.

CHAPTER FOUR

BRIAN spun away from her, looking towards the door.
His face reddened, his eyes widening, startled.

'Mind your own business,' he said sullenly.

Luke towered dangerously in the doorway. His
face was harsh, his eyes chips of ice as he looked at
Brian with obvious distaste. 'I don't think the lady
wants to be kissed,' he dropped the words with icy
menace at Brian's feet.

Brian glared at Luke for a long moment, hesitating
between doing what he was told or defying Luke.
Finally he pushed his hands into his pockets, his lip
curling in a sneer as he looked at Luke.

'Saving her for yourself, are you?' he jeered.

Luke's eyes glittered dangerously. His mouth was
compressed into a hard, uncompromising line, his
jaw taut with anger. His powerful, muscular body
blocked the doorway.

Kate looked at Brian. 'I think you'd better go,'
she said quickly, her hands shaking slightly with
delayed reaction.

'You'd like that, wouldn't you?' Brian said nastily.
'With me out of the way you'll have him all to yourself.'

Luke took a step towards him, his face looking as
though it was carved from granite, his eyes a brilliant
shade of blue, glinting icily as he looked at Brian.

'If you're not out of here in five seconds,' he said

in a flinty, clipped voice, 'I'll break your neck in three separate places.' He stood a few feet from Brian, danger emanating from him, every line of his hard, powerful body backing up his threat, making it crystal clear that he meant what he said.

Brian glared at him, then moved to walk past him. Luke's hand shot out, taking a vice-like hold of his arm.

'Hey!' Brian protested, shrinking away from him.

'Keep your mouth shut when you step outside the door,' Luke told him harshly, his eyes glittering menacingly.

Brian stared at him sullenly, 'All right, all right,' he muttered, keeping as far away from Luke as possible, 'I wasn't going to say anything to them.'

Luke watched him grimly. 'Don't try it. If you do, I'll come after you, and when I get you I'll take you apart piece by piece.'

He released Brian roughly, and turned his head slightly as Brian bolted out of the door and down the stairs, disappearing like a genie. He looked back at Kate. 'Are you okay?' he asked.

Kate nodded, feeling shaken and confused. 'Nothing broken,' she said quietly, 'except my faith in human nature.'

Luke smiled grimly. 'I'm sorry. I was afraid that might happen.' He watched her steadily, his eyes enigmatic.

She shrugged. 'That's okay. It isn't your fault. I just picked the wrong man.'

She looked at the floor with a dazed expression. This really wasn't her day. So much had happened to her within the space of twenty-four hours that she was left reeling, trying to take it all in.

She looked up at Luke, a question forming in her eyes. 'How did you know what was happening?' she asked.

He shrugged. 'I came out to help you bring in the coffee. I heard you tell him to get out and then there was a muffled silence. I wasn't sure if you'd want my interference or not.'

Kate smiled wryly. 'I'm glad you came in when you did. It wasn't a very pleasant experience.'

'I gathered that when I heard you cry out,' Luke told her drily.

Kate turned and picked up a cloth, taking the frantically boiling kettle off the gas and filling the cups with hot water. She smiled slightly at him. 'Well, now you're here, you can help me make the coffee.'

Luke chuckled, and went over to the fridge, getting the milk out. He handed it to her silently, and she pointed to the tray in the corner. 'Could you get that for me?' she asked.

Luke got her the tray and they put the coffee cups on it. 'How long had you known him?' Luke asked casually.

'Oh, only about a month,' she told him, 'but I'd been seeing him for two weeks, practically every other night.'

He watched her steadily, his blue eyes enigmatic. 'You must have got on pretty well together if you were seeing each other that much.'

Kate shrugged. 'Not really. It just happened, that's all. He was very nice to me, but I wasn't in love with him, and he certainly wasn't in love with me.'

Luke nodded, picking up the tray. He smiled. 'You go and get changed. I'll take these in.'

Kate watched him walk into the living room, closing the door behind him. He was like a Chinese puzzle; complex and difficult to understand.

She went into her bedroom and took her white woollen dress off its hanger, laying it on the bed. Then she went in the bathroom and washed quickly, wrapping a towel round her and going back into the bedroom.

Why must people be so complicated? she thought wearily. First Brian turned out to be a stranger, then he had attacked her, and finally, Luke came in at her defence. She frowned irritably. She had felt a surge of pride when Luke had spoken to Brian in that icy, menacing tone.

But Luke wasn't her man, he was just someone with whom she was stuck for the next couple of days. Not that she minded being stuck with him, she admitted to herself. But he was certainly having a strange effect on her.

Her feelings were very confused. She pushed all thoughts aside as she dressed quickly, brushing her hair until it shone, and finally slipping on her shoes. She paused before leaving the room, looking in the mirror.

She looked better than she had when she had got up. Her face had more colour to it, the creamy texture of her skin complementing her silky, raven black hair. She quickly put some mascara on her lashes and a touch of lipstick on her full mouth, making her look more alive.

Luke looked up as she entered the living room. His eyes ran over the length of her body, taking in the way the smooth white wool clung sensuously to her slim body. As his electric blue eyes flickered slowly back up to her face, she felt herself begin to blush slightly, and averted her eyes.

It was then that she noticed Luke was alone. She looked back at him, a puzzled frown on her face. 'Where are the others?' she asked.

'Lisa had to go straight back to the office to release the statement officially,' he told her casually.

'What about Linda?'

He smiled slightly, tilting his head towards the door on the other side of the room. Kate looked at the door, then back at him. His eyes were lit with sparks of amusement. 'I get the feeling she doesn't like me any more,' Luke told her drily.

Kate sighed. 'What did you say to her?' she asked wearily.

He shrugged. 'I asked her exactly what happened and why. When I made it plain that I wasn't pleased with her she stormed out with a sulky expression on her face.'

'You didn't shout at her?' Kate asked hopefully.

Luke raised his eyebrows in surprise. 'Of course I didn't,' he told her, his face perfectly straight.

Kate eyed him suspiciously. He was quite capable of looking her straight in the eye and lying. She went to the door of Linda's bedroom, pressing her ear against it and listening in case she was crying.

Silence prevailed within, and she tapped gently at the door. 'Linda!' she called brightly.

She heard a muffled movement inside. Then, 'Go

away,' said a sulky voice.

Kate sighed. 'Can I come in?' she asked in a cheerful voice, tapping on the door again. There was no reply. She looked over her shoulder at Luke, who was watching her with an amused expression. It was all very well him finding this funny, but she was the one who would have to live with Linda.

She tried the door and it opened. She put her head round the door, a bright smile affixed to her face. 'Mind if I come in?' she asked Linda.

Linda was sitting on the bed with a scowl on her face. She folded her hands on her lap and glared at Kate. 'What do you want?'

Kate went in the room, closing the door behind her firmly. 'I just wondered if you were okay,' she told Linda casually.

Linda snorted. 'Well, I'm fine,' she said crossly, her round blue eyes daring Kate to disagree with her. She sat back against the pillows, continuing to glare at Kate.

Kate leaned against the door. 'I'm going down to Keyford to see my family,' she told her, 'and I don't know exactly when I'll be back. I thought I'd better let you know where I was going before I went.'

Linda ignored this. 'Your Luke Hastings shouted at me,' she said accusingly.

Kate sighed wearily. She disliked her friend when she was in one of her moods, she became so childishly irritating. 'He isn't my Luke Hastings.'

'Well, you brought him here. It didn't occur to you that I might have been worried sick last night. How was I to know you'd come straight back here with him? I thought you'd been kidnapped or something!' Linda blurted the words out in one long string, her voice accusing.

'So I found out,' Kate said drily. She turned and opened the door, deciding to postpone the inevitable argument with Linda until she came back from her parents' house. 'I'll see you as soon as I get back.'

Linda merely glared at her, her lips jutting out stubbornly. Kate sighed and went out of the room, closing the door behind her wearily. Linda was proving herself almost impossible to live with. She threw Luke an irritated glance. 'Couldn't you have handled her rather more delicately?' she asked as they left the flat.

Luke raised one jet-black eyebrow sardonically. 'I thought I was remarkably patient with her.'

'Really?' Kate queried as Luke held the front door open for her, 'Then why is she sulking?'

Luke shrugged. 'I have no idea,' he told her blandly. They reached the outside front door, and Luke turned to her with a smile. 'Just stay with me and make for the car.'

Kate nodded, and waited as he opened the door. The crowds pushed forwards, and she hung on tight to Luke's wrist as they made their way to the car.

She managed to ignore the questions, the leering faces and the bright flash of the cameras as they aimed their lenses at her. It wasn't as unnerving as it had been before. Maybe I'm getting used to it, she thought drily as Luke put her in the car.

They drove away quickly, leaving the reporters disappointed at getting no answers from them. They had probably been waiting there since quite early that morning.

Luke turned to her as they passed out of the borders of the city. 'Whereabouts in Essex is it?' he asked, his voice deep and casual.

'Keyford. Do you know it?' she replied.

Luke nodded, slowing down as they came to a set of traffic lights. 'Yes, I know it. Not very well, but I know how to get there.' He paused, a frown crinkling his brow slightly. 'I seem to remember doing a concert near there a few years ago.'

Kate nodded, smiling. 'That's right. It was in the big hall a few miles away from Keyford.'

Luke pressed his foot on the clutch, the muscles in his thighs rippling beneath the black trousers as she did so. The car moved forward smoothly, gathering speed quickly. He grinned at Kate, glancing at her out of the corner of his eye. 'You must have been about twelve when I was there,' he teased, his eyes twinkling with amusement.

She chuckled. 'I was sixteen, actually,' she told him wryly.

Luke's eyebrows rose in surprise. 'So old?' he mocked lightly.

'Well, I'm twenty now,' Kate told him, looking out of the windscreen as they passed through the suburbs.

'Are you? I thought you were younger than that. You look about eighteen,' said Luke, his voice losing its mocking tone.

Kate grimaced. She had never looked older than she was, but she hadn't thought she looked as young as eighteen. She mentally chastised herself; she was only two years away from eighteen. It was just that eighteen seemed so young. It seemed as though she had left that age behind light years ago. She shrugged. Age was a state of mind, and when one was growing up, the stages passed quickly.

She lapsed into a steady silence, relaxing in the luxurious interior of the car as they sped towards their destination. The familiar streets flashed by, reminding her of her earlier visits to and from London when she was still living at home. A smile touched her lips as she pictured her family driving up to London for the day in the car, her parents in the front, and herself and Graham in the back.

Graham was her younger brother by eighteen months, and they would squabble all the way to London and back, with her mother turning her head absently from time to time, asking them to be quiet. She missed her family. But that was only to be expected in the first few months of leaving home.

She wondered how they were taking the news of her supposed kidnap. They wouldn't believe it to be as serious as the papers made it seem, but they would definitely be worried. She was glad Luke was taking her down there. It was always easier to explain something delicate if one was face to face instead of just speaking through a telephone receiver.

Luke was slowing the car down to a steady thirty miles an hour. Kate looked up at the streets, realising that they were still a long way from Keyford. She frowned. 'Why are we slowing down?'

Luke glanced at his watch. 'We can't drop in on your family at lunchtime. I thought we'd stop here for something to eat. I know a very good restaurant in this particular town. I don't want to spend hours looking for somewhere else once we've passed through.'

Kate eyed the silent clock on the dashboard. It was half-past twelve, she realised with surprise.

'It's small, but the food's very good,' Luke told her as he stepped out of the car a moment later.

Kate got out and looked with pleasure at the small, homely restaurant with the brown striped canopy and a small glass front. She wrapped her coat protectively around herself. It was quite cold still and the warmth of the car was in direct contrast to the atmosphere outside.

They walked inside the restaurant to be greeted by the head waiter, who beamed effusively at them. He fussed over Luke, obviously pleased that he had chosen to revisit the restaurant.

Kate watched with a wry smile on her lips. She liked this place, she decided. It had a very discreet atmosphere, quiet and luxurious. The only other customers were two very old men who ignored Luke and Kate's presence, continuing with what appeared to be a business discussion.

They sat down and Luke smiled at her wryly as the waiter disappeared. 'I didn't think they'd remember me,' he told her with amusement. 'I haven't been here for three years.'

Kate laughed softly. 'They were hardly likely to forget you,' she pointed out.

Luke shrugged, bending his well-shaped black head to study the menu. Kate studied his bent head for a moment, feeling a strange sense of intimacy at dining out with him in this quiet little restaurant. She watched his eyes flickering over the menu, noticing how very thick his sooty black lashes were as they rested against his tanned skin.

It was strange how her feelings towards him were so conflicting, she thought with a slight frown as she read her own menu. On the one hand, she was very much aware of him as a vitally attractive stranger. On the other hand, she sometimes felt as though she had known him all her life.

He had only entered her life last night, but he had immediately become very much a part of her world.

The waiter reappeared with their drinks, took their orders, then disappeared once more as though in a puff of smoke.

Kate sipped the cool Martini, swirling the glass around and watching with a frown as the ice clinked against the sides. What would the meeting with her parents be like? she wondered.

'Don't look so worried,' Luke told her calmly. 'Linda hasn't said anything dangerous. No one's going to question our story.'

She looked up in surprise. 'I wasn't thinking about that.'

He raised one eyebrow. 'I see. In that case, why the frown?'

She shrugged. 'No reason. I was just thinking, that's all.' She noticed the glint in his eye, and expounded, 'About my parents—I'm a bit worried about how they're going to take all this.'

Luke watched her steadily. 'Are they likely to make a fuss?' he asked, his face expressionless.

She frowned. 'I don't think so. But I wouldn't want to take bets on it. They can be pretty unpredictable at the best of times. My mother's very easy-going, but my father's rather conventional.'

He nodded, picking up the long glass from the table and sipping the ice-cool lager. Kate fiddled absently with the cutlery. She looked at her watch. What time would they eventually arrive at her family's house? They must be very worried about her—they hadn't heard from her yet. She should really have rung them before they left Luke's house.

It was possible they had left the house to come up to the city and find out exactly what was going on. Kate looked at Luke from beneath her lashes.

'I think I should ring them,' she said quietly.

He studied her for a long moment from beneath heavy lids, then he nodded. 'I think there's a phone over there,' he told her, pushing his chair back. He stood up with a fluid, graceful movement, his long legs straightening.

Kate stood up too, and began to walk past him in the direction of the phone. 'There's no need for you to come with me,' she told him with a smile.

Luke stopped her, his hand clamping over her arm, and she looked up at him with a puzzled expression. He studied her with piercing blue eyes, his face enigmatic.

'Perhaps not,' he said in a dark voice, 'but I'll still come with you.' He towered over her, his height and muscular power somehow menacing as she felt the mood change between them.

'I'm only going to tell them we're on our way,' she told him, her brows linked together in a frown.

Luke's hand tightened fractionally on her arm, the long fingers hurting her flesh. 'I said I'll come with you.'

Kate shrugged, wondering what on earth was the matter with him. 'Okay, if you really want to.'

Luke walked with her, his hand still on her arm, releasing her only when they reached the telephone. Kate picked up the receiver with one hand, the other hand rummaging in her bag for a coin, but Luke handed her one while she was in mid-search. 'Thank you,' she said, closing her handbag and beginning to dial the number.

The phone rang for a long time before it was picked up. She slipped the money in as she heard the harsh notes of the pips.

A guarded voice recited the number, and Kate recognised it immediately. 'Hello,' she said cheerfully, 'it's me.'

'Who's me?' asked the voice suspiciously.

Kate laughed. 'Me. Kate.'

There was a sigh of relief as her mother finally recognised her voice.

'Katherine!' her mother said worriedly. 'What on earth have you been getting up to? We've had reporters from the local papers ringing up all morning wanting to know if you've been in touch.'

'Didn't you read the papers?' she asked her mother, feeling somewhat surprised.

'Oh yes, dear. But I didn't think it was true.' Kate heard muffled shouts in the background and grinned, recognising Graham's voice. Her mother told Graham to go away and stop shouting. 'Where was I?' her mother mused thoughtfully.

'You didn't think it was true,' Kate reminded her. Really, her mother was so absentminded it was becoming absurd!

'That's right. Well, we read the papers, and at first we were worried. But I said to your father, "Kate's got more sense than to get involved with someone like him." '

Kate laughed, looking at Luke out of the corner of her eye. He was watching her with an expressionless face. 'Listen,' she said quickly to her mother, 'I'll be down there in about an hour and a half.'

'Stop it, Graham,' her mother said wearily. 'Sorry, Kate, I didn't hear you. Graham's making a nuisance of himself, as usual.'

Kate grinned. 'I said I'll be down in about an hour and a half,' she told her mother. 'We're just having something to eat.'

'Did you say "we"?' her mother asked suspiciously.

'Yes. Luke Hastings is with me.'

'Oh, goodness, is he really?' Her mother sounded worried. 'Well, I won't tell anyone. Better leave it as a surprise. Get off, Graham, there's a good boy. Go and play with your bike.'

'I'll see you when I get there, then,' said Kate.

'Katherine,' her mother paused, 'you are all right, aren't you? I mean, it wasn't true, was it?'

Kate smiled, hearing the genuine note of concern in her mother's voice. 'Yes, I'm fine. I'll see you soon. 'Bye!'

'Goodbye, dear,' her mother said as she hung up.

Kate turned to Luke with a smile. 'Everything's okay,' she told him brightly.

'Good,' he said curtly.

Kate made a face. Miserable pig! She walked back to the table, seeing the dishes waiting for them, and sat down to eat. She was amazed at how hungry she was. All that action this morning on an empty stomach, she thought with a smile.

As she finished her meal, she picked up her glass and finished the delicately flavoured wine, glancing at Luke as she did so. He'd been very quiet all through the meal, eating and drinking silently while she chattered on about her family.

Her brows linked together in a puzzled frown as she recalled the way he had behaved when she had told him she was making the call to her family. Luke was leaning back in his chair, an unlit cigar in his hand. He looked at her with enigmatic blue eyes.

'Do you mind if I smoke?' he asked casually. At her reply, he took out a slim gold lighter, holding the flame to the tip. Silver-blue smoke floated from the glowing tip of the cigar as he drew on it.

Kate leaned forward. 'Why did you want to come to the phone with me?' she asked in a puzzled voice.

Luke shrugged, his eyes hooded, half hidden as a haze of cigar smoke rose in front of his face. He rested the cigar in the ashtray and sipped his coffee.

She studied him with her head tilted to one side. He had been quite definite about coming to the phone with her. In fact, he had made it plain that he wasn't going to let her out of his sight.

'Did you want to talk to my parents?' she asked, watching him very closely.

He shrugged once more, looking up, but not quite meeting her eyes, and Kate frowned. There was something funny here. He was behaving very strangely about this.

'Luke,' she said slowly, her eyes narrowing as an

idea came into her head, 'why didn't you want me to go to the phone on my own?'

Luke drew on his cigar, then summoned the waiter to their table to ask for the bill. Kate watched him suspiciously. What was he hiding?

'Aren't you going to answer me?' she asked in a controlled voice, staring at him as he continued to avoid her eyes and ignore her. He took some notes from his pocket and began counting them out, a bland expression on his face. Kate watched him, beginning to feel angry at the way he was ignoring her.

'Luke,' she said through tight lips, 'I am talking to you. Would you mind answering my question?'

He looked up. 'We'll discuss it in the car,' he said in a calm voice, putting the notes on the saucer with the bill.

Her lips compressed into a tight line. 'We'll discuss it now,' she said jerkily.

'Leave it,' he said brusquely, turning his head to summon the waiter once more.

Kate felt the indignation rise inside her. She knew exactly why he had insisted on coming to the phone with her. He had thought she was going to ring up the press and deny the story he and Lisa had released. He still believed she was responsible for all that had happened.

She watched him with angry eyes, feeling her fists clench into tight little balls. She struggled to hold on to her temper. Luke was treating her unfairly. She was sick of his accusations, and to actually believe she was capable of such sneaky behaviour made her blood boil.

'You thought I was ringing the press, didn't you?' she asked tightly, and had the gratification of seeing a tinge of deep red colour his face. 'What the hell do you think I am?' she snapped at him across the table. 'Some kind of Mata Hari?'

His brows jerked together in a frown. 'I said leave it,' he bit out.

Kate pushed back her chair and stood up abruptly. 'I will not leave it!' she said angrily.

His hand shot out and caught her wrist. 'Sit down!'

Out of the corner of her eye she noticed that the other two customers were now staring curiously towards their table. She gave Luke a blistering smile. 'So sorry. Am I embarrassing you?'

His mouth clamped shut like a steel trap, and he stood up, his hand still holding on to her wrist. 'Sit down,' he demanded tightly.

She glared at him, her eyes flashing with the force of her anger. 'Why the hell should I?' she spat, her back arched like that of a furious kitten, then turned quickly and ran out of the restaurant, leaving Luke staring angrily after her, his eyes stabbing at her.

CHAPTER FIVE

As she swung out of the glass doors, her eyes darted frantically from side to side, seeking an avenue of escape. She shivered, realising with dismay that she had left her coat in the restaurant. She began to walk briskly down the little high street, casting furtive glances over her shoulder in case Luke was following her.

It would have been easier to bear, she thought, if she had actually had something to do with all this mess. But she had been totally innocent right from the start. She had had enough of Luke's accusations for one day. He must think he's some kind of omnipotent god, she thought bitterly as she wrapped her arms around herself in an effort to keep warm.

She heard the car door slam from a distance, and quickened her footsteps. Now he was coming after her. Well, she thought crossly, what did I expect? There was no way she was going to be able to avoid him. She broke into a run.

The wheels of the sleek black sports car screeched to a halt just in front of her, and Luke got out of the car, his jet black hair lifted slightly in the chill winter breeze.

'Get in,' he ordered angrily, his hand resting on the door.

Kate ignored him, trying to walk past, but his hand shot out and caught her shoulder, yanking her

back unceremoniously. She landed against the solid
wall of his chest.

'Take your filthy hands off me!' she said in a low,
angry voice.

His eyes were blazingly angry, his hard mouth
compressed into a thin line as he stared down at her.
'I said, get in the car,' he bit out between strong
teeth.

'Go to hell!' she snapped, her green eyes spitting
with angry defiance.

His strong arms tightened round her like steel
bands. He pushed her into the car and closed the
door, then came round to his side, sliding in next to
her, his face grim.

'Who the hell do you think you are?' she
demanded, 'pushing me about like this?'

Luke started the car, every line of his body tensed
with unleashed anger. 'Shut up!' he snapped.

Kate's lips tightened. She pushed at the door
handle, but he had locked it from the dashboard.
Tears of impotent rage hovered behind her eyes,
pricking her lids. Her lower lip trembled as she
fought back the desire to hit him.

'I'm sick and tired of listening to your insults,' she
burst out as the car began to pull away from the
kerb, 'and I'm sick and tired of the way you man-
handle me every time I object to your accusations!'

Luke's hands tightened on the steering wheel, his
knuckles showing white against his tanned skin. He
stared straight ahead of him, a muscle jerking in his
cheek, his mouth hard and forbidding.

'You thought I was ringing the press, didn't you?'
she snapped, but Luke didn't reply.

His face was harsh, as though it had been carved out of granite. He jerked the car viciously into gear.

'Didn't you?' she shouted angrily.

His head jerked round, his eyes black with anger. 'Yes,' he snarled, his lips drawn back over his teeth.

'I wasn't phoning them, though. And you damned well know it,' she said in a low, trembling voice. 'But you're not going to apologise, are you?'

He remained silent, manoeuvring the car swiftly around a long country lane. Every line in his body spelt danger, but Kate was far too angry with him to take any notice of it. He had been at her throat all day, and she had had just about all she could take.

Her hands balled into tight fists at her sides. 'I don't even rate an apology, do I?'

Luke glanced across at her, his black brows menacing above his autocratic nose. Fury was written in his dark eyes, his skin taut across his strong cheekbones. He didn't answer her, but the car put on speed convulsively, and Kate felt herself being forced back in her seat by the sudden spurt of speed.

She felt the anger boil up inside her like a volcanic eruption. She looked at his harsh profile with hatred, indignation and rage welling up until she could barely control it.

'You bastard!' she said in a shaking voice, her fists tensed at her sides. 'You low, stinking bastard!' Her voice began to rise with sheer fury towards the end, until she was almost screaming the words at him.

His mouth shut like a steel trap. The car screeched to a halt on the narrow country lane, throwing up gravel as it did so. Kate was thrown forwards in her seat, only to be snapped back by the seat belt, her head thrown back like a whipcrack.

He turned to her, his eyes blazing, his skin white against his harsh bones. His hands pulled his seat belt off quickly, his hard body poised with tension.

Kate felt the first tremors of fear. She looked wildly around her, but there was no one in sight. They were surrounded by fields. She looked back at him with wide eyes.

'You scheming little witch!' he growled in a dark voice that hovered dangerously between rage and self-control. His hands took her shoulders suddenly, dragging her towards him. He moved across to her, his fingers biting into the soft flesh of her upper arms.

Kate's heart fluttered wildly against her chest as she tried to push him away, but her flimsy attempts were totally ineffectual. His black head swooped until he was practically touching her face with his.

'My God, you've been asking for this,' he snarled, his lips drawn back over his teeth as his mouth clamped over hers.

The kiss was brutal, punishing, his mouth moving harshly against hers, forcing her lips back until she wanted to scream, and she tasted the salty flow of tears on her mouth.

His hands were on her back, pressing her against his hard chest until she felt the breath being squeezed out of her. She tried to put her hands up to push him away, but they were trapped against him, and he wouldn't budge.

More hot tears pricked behind her eyelids as he held her. She struggled, but his arms tightened

around her like steel bands. His lips hurt her, hard
and firm as they punished the soft skin of her mouth.
He clamped one hand on her neck when she tried to
move her head away from his face.

Kate felt as though she was being strangled. The
car and the scenery outside began to fade and blur as
she fought to control the situation that seemed totally
beyond her.

Suddenly the kiss changed. Luke's hands softened
on her, his mouth becoming less demanding. His lips
teased hers gently, evoking a response deep inside
her.

His hot mouth moved sensuously against hers. His
hands slid down her back, making her shiver from
her head right down to her toes. She found herself
pressing against him, her soft, warm body pliant in
his arms.

His mouth left hers and moved down to her neck,
licking the soft skin with his tongue, sending sharp
sensations through her. His strong teeth nibbled her
throat, and her heart began beating fiercely against
her breastbone as her mind lost control and her body
took over.

His mouth moved back up, his hot breath fanning
her ear as his tongue licked at the sensitive skin of
her lobe. Kate shivered, pressing against him, and
her body began to glow with heat as she sought and
found his mouth, and passion flared between them.

His long fingers slid sensuously round her waist,
stroking her stomach while his mouth drugged her
with his kiss. His fingers began to slide slowly, tantalisingly upwards. Kate arched towards him, needing to feel his strong hands close over her breasts.

She didn't understand this aching need which was beginning to take over. Her mind swam as common sense fought sexuality and lost the battle. She gave in to the demands of her body, her hands moving over his shoulders to tangle her fingers in his thick black hair.

His hands cupped her breasts and she groaned with pleasure, her breath coming faster, her pulses pounding all over her body.

Luke drew his head back, looking down at her with eyes which were black with desire. His breathing was accelerated, his heart thudding hard.

'Touch me,' he whispered hoarsely, and bent his black head once more, claiming her lips with a slow, drugging passion.

She moved her hands experimentally, running them slowly over his hard shoulder-blades, down to his chest. She felt the fierce crash of his heart against her hand as she stroked his chest lightly.

He stopped kissing her, drawing back, breathing thickly, watching her with eyes filled with desire. She looked back at him dumbly, her face hot with passion as she continued stroking his chest.

She undid a button, her eyes on him all the time, and slipped her hand inside his shirt. His flesh was hot under her palm. She undid another button, and another, staring at the smooth, tanned flesh in front of her.

Luke's breath was coming faster, his heart crashing maniacally against his ribcage. As she pulled his shirt open and stroked him with both hands, he drew his breath in sharply.

She looked up at his face. Her hands stroked his

chest, her nails scratching softly against his flesh, tangling in the short black hairs on his skin.

He made a strangled noise in the back of his throat. 'Yes,' he groaned thickly. 'Oh God, Kate, yes!'

His head swooped down on her, his eyes glittering with desire. She gave in to the demands of his kiss, returning the passion which she felt, responding as though he was a magician.

A loud noise brought them apart. The car flashed past them, flashing its lights and hooting loudly. Kate was startled into common sense. She put her hands to her hot cheeks, shame pouring through her, then looked at Luke, seeing his shirt open, his powerful chest exposed.

She shrank with embarrassment against the door of the car. She had only known him a short while. How could she have allowed herself to behave like that?

He turned back to her, frowning as he noticed the way she was pressed up against her side of the car. He reached out for her.

'It's all right,' he murmured. 'They've gone.'

Kate shook her head vigorously. 'It's not all right,' she told him quietly. 'I'm sorry.'

His brows jerked together, his blue eyes narrowing. 'What do you mean, you're sorry?' he asked slowly.

She swallowed nervously. 'I'm sorry,' she said, 'I've never behaved like that before. I don't know what came over me. It won't happen again.'

'It will if I have anything to say about it,' he told her with a lazy smile, his arm reaching over for her.

She pushed his hand away. 'Please don't,' she said through dry lips.

Luke frowned, his black brows drawn together over his autocratic nose. 'What the hell are you playing at?' he demanded.

Kate swallowed nervously. 'I'm not playing at anything. I'm simply asking you not to kiss me again.'

Luke swore under his breath, his face becoming harsh and smooth, as though it had been carved out of granite. 'Are you trying to tell me,' he said in a low, angry voice, 'that you didn't enjoy what we did just now?'

Kate blinked. She had two choices. If she told him the truth, that she had enjoyed it, he would try to carry on where they had left off. If she told him a lie, he would be very, very angry. She took a deep breath.

'I didn't enjoy it,' she whispered, looking him straight in the eye and hoping she sounded convincing.

His teeth clamped together, 'You lying witch,' he growled.

Kate shuddered at the violence in his tone. Her face went red with shame, turning white as a sheet after only a few seconds as she looked at Luke's angry eyes. They glittered down at her, pinning her to her seat.

His eyes narrowed speculatively. 'Is this a new strategy, Kate? Have you decided to catch me any way you can? Is this little episode calculated to have me on my knees with sexual hunger?'

Kate winced as he sniped the words at her. Her

face was completely white, her eyes large and frightened. 'Please don't make this difficult for me,' she
pleaded with him.

'Difficult for you?' he grated, staring at her with
anger glinting in the depths of his blue eyes. 'If
you're trying to tell me you're not used to this kind
of situation, you can forget it. I don't believe the
inexperienced act you put on, I don't believe it for a
second. You're used to this, all right; you're nothing
but a little tease!'

Kate flinched at the icy tone of his voice, as he
dropped the words like icicles at her feet. 'I'm sorry,'
she whispered, not quite meeting his eyes. She was
frightened of what she might see in them.

'You're not sorry!' Luke flung at her, his eyes con-
temptuous. He started the car, jerking it into gear
viciously, and they pulled away at speed, the wheels
spinning as he tried to force them into a speed they
were not yet capable of producing.

Kate bit her lip miserably, feeling a complete fool.
She had made him think the worst of her by her
behaviour. She had dug her own grave. She gazed
dismally out of the windows, watching the fields flash
past with painful clarity.

Luke turned to look at her, his eyes chips of ice.
'When this is all over, I'll find out if you were behind
it or not. If you planned all this, let me warn you,
Kate, I'll break your beautiful neck!'

Kate shivered; she had not missed the underlying
thread of violence in his icy voice. The sooner she
said goodbye to Luke Hastings and all he stood for,
the better. Thank God she would soon be home with
her family. She would feel a lot safer with them,

even if Luke was going to be there too.

They drove on in a steady silence. Kate passed the time by counting how many orange cars she saw on the roads. She didn't want to think, she was afraid of the pain she might feel if she allowed herself to dig too deep.

As they arrived in Keyford, Luke asked her for directions in a flat, unfriendly voice. She told him dully where she lived, and they carried on in silence.

They pulled up outside her family's house, and Kate heaved a sign of relief, stepping out of the car as quickly as she could and leaving Luke to lock it.

She almost tripped over the dirty heap of a motorcycle outside the front garden, but she smiled at it, and shook her head. Graham hadn't changed much. His first and last love was his motorcycle.

The front door was opened before she reached it, and a curly brown head popped round it, attached to a long, thin, gangly body which belonged to her brother Graham.

'Hello, ugly,' said Graham cheerfully. 'What have you been up to, then? Running off with strange men in the middle of the night?'

Kate grinned, her eyes sweeping over the uniform faded jeans and sneakers he wore, the T-shirt and jacket which had seen better days. 'Hello, Graham,' she said, her eyes scanning his cheerful, open face, the cheeky brown eyes that stared back at her. She gestured towards the motorcycle. 'I see you've still got that awful machine.'

Graham eyed her with disdain. 'Haven't you got eyes?' he enquired. 'That's a new one. Cost me a packet.'

Kate raised her eyebrows. 'I would have thought they'd have paid you to take it off their hands,' she teased, grinning.

He watched her with narrowed eyes for a second, then laughed, patting her on the head. 'Blind as a bat, you are,' he said, chuckling. He leaned forwards from his stance against the doorjamb. 'Here, is that the man of the moment?'

She turned to see Luke approaching them, and a wave of unaccountable sadness washed over her, but she pushed the feeling away, turning back to her brother. 'Yes, that's Luke.'

He raised a mischievous eyebrow. 'On first name terms now, are we?' he teased as Luke reached them. 'Hello,' he said, smiling at Luke. 'I'm Graham.' He offered him his hand.

Luke shook his hand with a smile. 'Glad to meet you. I'm Luke Hastings. Call me Luke.'

Graham frowned. 'Luke Hastings?' he murmured with mock thoughtfulness. 'Name rings a bell,' then he grinned, to show he was only teasing.

They went into the house, and Kate hung her coat over the newel post while Luke and Graham chatted. As she turned round, she saw her mother wandering out of the kitchen in their direction, wiping her hands on a tea-towel, and Kate grinned at her.

'Katherine,' Mrs Scott said in a warm voice, 'thank God you're home! We've had so much trouble telling everyone it isn't true, but you know what people are like.' She leant forward and kissed her daughter's cheek.

Kate smiled. 'I hope you haven't had too much

trouble. I've had enough at my end for all of us.'

Mrs Scott smiled, her calm blue eyes crinkling at the edges, her slightly podgy hands still dabbing aimlessly at the tea-towel. She was wearing her customary plastic pinny over the top of a dark brown dress which had specks of flour on it. She glanced down at it, absently dusting the flour off with the tea-towel.

'Well now,' she said, looking at Luke, 'you must be Mr Hastings.'

Luke smiled lazily, his eyes twinkling with charm, and took her podgy hand in his long tanned hand. 'I'm very pleased to meet you. Please call me Luke.'

'Well, Luke, why don't you and Kate come into the living room while I make the tea?'

Luke accepted this offer of tea charmingly, and followed Mrs Scott and Kate into the living room. Graham quickly sprawled into an armchair, watching with mischievous eyes as Kate was forced to sit next to Luke on the sofa.

Mrs Scott watched them with a benign smile. 'Would anyone like some cakes?' she asked calmly.

Graham groaned before anyone could answer 'Not Mrs Plumley's rock cakes!' he pleaded, holding his hands to his stomach.

Mrs Scott swiped him gently with the tea-towel. 'Hush, Graham, you evil child! You know very well that Mrs Plumley makes lovely rock cakes.'

'She's gonna make us some rock cakes we can't refuse,' Graham said, tapping an imaginary cigar. He gave Luke and Kate a lopsided grin. 'Rock being the operative word.'

Mrs Scott tutted and shook her head at him. She

turned back to Luke. 'I'll get you some of my own cream cakes,' she promised him with a motherly smile. Mrs Scott had strong maternal leanings towards anyone who was under fifty.

Luke smiled with charm. 'That sounds lovely, Mrs Scott.'

Mrs Scott beamed, and turned back to Graham. 'Come along, dear,' she said absently, 'help me with the wiping up.'

Graham pulled a face. 'Oh, Mum, I wanted to talk to Luke.' He glanced pleadingly at Kate for assistance, but Kate merely smiled back at him and kept silent.

Mrs Scott eased him out of his armchair with one hand and patted his arm with the other. 'Come on, dear. Many hands make light work, or something like that.'

Graham looked glum, but went out of the living room before her. Kate called her mother back. 'Where's Daddy?' she asked, realising for the first time that he was nowhere to be seen.

Mrs Scott waved her hand benignly. 'Oh, he's out with Sergeant Humphrey,' she told her.

Out of the corner of her eye, Kate saw Luke's narrowed eyes, his expression of anger, and felt her blood begin to boil again. She knew what was on his mind. He was beginning to distrust her again.

When the door was closed and they were alone again, Luke turned to her, his jawline straight with anger. 'Who,' he asked between his teeth, 'is Sergeant Humphrey?'

Kate eyed him with disdain. Who the hell did he think he was? He couldn't believe for one second that she might be a totally innocent bystander in all this mess. Everything, it appeared, that surrounded or had anything to do with her was automatically suspect.

Luke's blue eyes flashed ominously. 'I asked you a question,' he said tautly.

She turned towards him, controlling her anger, forcing a sweet smile to her lips. 'Sergeant Humphrey,' she told him in a voice like melted honey, 'is an old friend of the family.'

He watched her steadily, his black head held rigid. 'And what is he doing talking with your father today?' he asked, his deep, crisp voice filled with accusation and suspicion.

Kate's hands clenched into fists. She wanted to bat him over the head with something. She had never before met anyone so intolerably suspicious. 'How on earth should I know?' she asked tightly. 'Perhaps they've just gone out for a quiet drink.'

Luke frowned, and shook his head. 'Try again, Kate. It's too coincidental that they should be out today of all days.'

Kate stood up and wandered over to the window, looking out on the village she had once lived in. She didn't want to discuss this with Luke any more. He was being ridiculous. She pulled back the lace curtain slightly and peered across the road. The same old houses were there, with the same people still living in them.

Yet Kate felt oddly out of place, as though she was now an outsider. It wasn't merely living away from home for a month that made her feel that way, she knew that. It was meeting Luke, and seeing the vast gulf between them. Seeing how very different their life-styles were, and realising that she had lived in so small a world before, with a very narrow view of outside influences.

She turned her head as she felt him come to stand next to her. He was watching her with those piercing blue eyes, as though he was trying to see right through into her mind, read all her thoughts. She shivered.

They both looked out of the window just as a car drew up and three men got out, one of them holding a camera. Not again! thought Kate. Why can't they leave us alone?

Luke pulled her away from the window quickly, his arms going around her shoulders. 'That was pretty stupid,' he remarked bitingly.

Kate frowned. 'What's that supposed to mean? I was only looking out of my own front window. How was I to know they'd send the ravening hounds over here?'

'It should have occurred to you,' Luke told her brusquely, his hands still resting on her shoulders as he spoke. 'News travels fast. Someone must have telephoned the press as soon as we arrived.'

She compressed her lips, biting back a sharp retort. Why did he always have to blame her for everything? She sighed, her eyes wandering back to look out of the window. They obviously hadn't seen them there, or they would have come closer to the house.

Luke pursed his hard lips thoughtfully. 'More will follow, of course. The place will be overrun by reporters in no time at all.'

Kate eyed him with dislike. The tone of his voice made it obvious that he still blamed her for all that had happened. She gave him a blistering smile. 'You're the one who's famous, not me,' she pointed out. 'If you'd been a dustman, none of this would have happened.'

His hands tightened slightly on her shoulder, and she glanced down at the lean brown fingers.

'How true,' he said unpleasantly. 'But if I had been a dustman, you wouldn't have hurt your ankle so conveniently.'

Kate's lips tightened further. She glanced at the reporters who skulked outside the window. 'By the time you leave,' she told him tightly, 'there'll be millions of reporters out there. You're like the Pied Piper—you attract rats.'

Luke looked at her in disbelief for a moment. Then his eyes narrowed, his face taking on a menacing look. His hands tightened on her shoulders, pulling her closer to him. 'Don't push your luck too far, Kate,' he threatened in a crisp voice.

She backed imperceptibly, afraid of what he might do, but at that moment the door opened, and Graham came in with a tray of cakes.

'Hello, hello, hello,' he said, his eyes sweeping over them as they stood in the middle of the room.

Luke's hands dropped from her shoulders. He raked a hand through his thick black hair and gestured towards the front garden. 'There are some reporters out there,' he said.

Graham chuckled, winking mischievously at Kate. 'That's your story and you're sticking to it,' he said, putting the tray down on the table next to the sofa.

Luke glowered at Kate, who simply ignored him and took her place on the sofa. Mrs Scott entered with a pot of steaming hot tea and some cups and saucers. She set them down on the table and beamed at Luke.

'I'll be mum, shall I?' she said, picking up the teapot and pouring his tea. 'Here you are,' she handed it to him with another smile.

Luke began to talk to Graham and Mrs Scott, recounting funny stories about the pop world in which he made his living. Graham appeared to be fascinated with these stories, listening intently, leaning forward with a wide smile on his face.

After fifteen minutes, they all heard the key in the lock of the front door, followed by angry mutterings. Graham pulled a face. 'The master of the house is home,' he announced.

The sitting room door opened, and a large, very fat labrador bounded into the room, panting and wagging his tail. He pounced on Mrs Scott, licking her all over her face, his tail thumping on the floor.

Then he bounced on Graham, who ruffled his neck and said, 'Hello, Tubby. Been eating too much today, have you?'

The dog went over to Luke and sniffed at him inquisitively. Luke patted his head.

Kate tried to keep the smile out of her voice as she said, 'This is our old friend Sergeant Humphrey.'

Luke's hand stopped in mid-air, his face taking on a stunned look. He turned to Kate. 'This,' he said in amazement,' is Sergeant Humphrey?'

Kate nodded, her eyes twinkling with laughter.

'We call him Humph for short.'

Luke stared at her in disbelief for a second, then he burst out laughing. 'Why didn't you tell me?' he said, his voice deep with humour.

Kate grinned. 'You didn't stop to ask if it was a dog. You just assumed the worst as usual.'

His blue eyes twinkled with amusement. Then his expression sobered, and he took her hand gently underneath one of the cushions. 'I'm sorry,' he said quietly, his eyes holding hers. 'I should think before I speak.'

She raised an eyebrow. 'Never was a truer word spoken,' she told him, then she smiled.

Luke shook his head, his hand gently holding hers. Something changed in the atmosphere between them, some expression changing in his eyes. Kate felt her breath catch in her throat. She turned away, averting her eyes, feeling suddenly frightened by the depth of emotion which had hit her at that moment.

A movement to her right caught her eye and she looked up to see her father watching them. His black hair was still thick, even though he was forty-five, his hazel eyes still alert and intelligent. Both Kate and Graham respected him immensely. He ruled the house with a proverbial iron hand in velvet glove. He was always firm, and tried to be fair, but if he was disobeyed, he would come down very hard on the person concerned.

She stood up slowly, holding out her hands, her eyes and smile warm. 'Hello, Daddy.'

Mr Scott looked at her blankly for a moment. He had been deeply shocked and worried by the newspaper stories. He had worried for his daughter's

safety at the hands of Luke Hastings. Now he was
overwhelmed with relief that she was safely home.

'Katherine!' He smiled and took her hands,
squeezing them gently as he kissed her cheek. 'Well,'
he said briskly as he caught Graham and Mrs Scott
watching him with indulgent smiles, 'it's good to
have you home again.' He cleared his throat and
shoved his hands into his pockets.

Luke stood up, his face hard and expressionless, as
though he wasn't sure of his reception from Mr
Scott.

Mr Scott looked at him with a cold face. 'Is this
the man concerned?' he enquired in a hard voice.

Luke nodded. Kate looked at him quickly. 'This
is Luke Hastings, Daddy,' she told him, hoping that
there wouldn't be any trouble.

Mr Scott glanced at her for a moment. He looked
back at Luke with narrowed eyes, his expression
giving nothing away, then nodded. 'Mr Hastings.'

Luke watched him steadily. 'Mr Scott,' he nodded
back.

Mr Scott turned and gave his wife a speaking
glance, which Mrs Scott clearly received and understood, because she looked at her children and said,
'Come along, you can help me clear away the tea
things.'

They left the room quietly, leaving Luke and
Kate's father facing each other in a stony silence.
Kate bit her lip anxiously. She hoped that Luke
would be able to persuade her father that nothing
had happened between them. She felt a hot rush of
colour as she realised that that wouldn't be quite
correct. But nothing had taken place last night, she

thought, trying to ease her conscience a little.

She didn't want to imagine the situation if her father refused to believe him. He could be extremely frightening at times, although he was never violent. She just hoped his sense of fair play would rescue the situation and make him see the truth.

She wandered into the kitchen, her mind spinning with thoughts. Graham tapped her on the shoulder as she walked past.

'Don't worry,' he said cheerfully, 'the end of the world isn't nigh.'

Kate looked up, her eyes puzzled, her brows linked in a frown. 'Sorry, I missed that. What did you say?'

Graham handed her a tea-towel. 'You look bootfaced. A little healthy exercise will be just the thing you need. You wipe, I'll watch.'

Kate laughed softly. 'Lazybones!' she admonished, as Graham made himself comfortable on the wooden stool in the kitchen. Mrs Scott continued washing the plates with an absent look on her face, handing them to Kate to dry up with the cloth.

'Come on, then,' Graham said cheerfully, grinning at her across the room, 'spill the beans. Tell all!'

'Which particular beans were you thinking of?' Kate asked, trying to avoid what she could see was coming.

Graham tutted, and picked at a small hole in his jeans. 'You know very well. I want to know what happened.'

Kate raised an eyebrow and crossed the room to place a glass precariously on the shelf. 'It isn't an instalment of *Crossroads*, you know,' she told him with a slight smile.

Graham shook his head and strolled over to the corner of the room, picking up a rather dirty-looking crash helmet. He took a cloth from the sink and sat down again, beginning to clean the crash helmet. 'Go on, Kate. I'm interested.'

Mrs Scott spotted the missing cloth and took it from him, pinching his nose as she did so. 'Don't use my cloths on your filthy old hats!'

Graham sighed. 'It's not a hat, it's a helmet,' he explained patiently, then turned back to Kate.

'Why should you be interested?' Kate asked before he could speak. She deliberately kept her voice as calm as possible. She didn't want to talk about the last twenty-four hours—she didn't feel up to it. So much had happened, and some of it was very upsetting. She could understand Graham's curiosity, but she did wish he would stop asking.

Graham grinned. 'Because I'm going to sell my story to the *News of the World*. "My Sister—How She Was Pillaged by Luke Hastings".'

Kate shook her head, her hand slowing as she dried a saucer. Was she being rather selfish? Did her parents want her to tell them about her experiences? Her mother didn't seem to mind that much, but perhaps she was merely waiting until Kate felt she could tell her in her own time.

She sighed. 'Oh, very well,' she said, putting the cloth down. She changed her mind and picked it back up again. Perhaps she would feel better if she had something to do while she was talking—it might make it easier.

Graham sat and listened avidly as she spoke, carefully skirting round the parts which would upset her, or cut too deeply. As she spoke, she realised how vivid everything had been since she met Luke. Her life before yesterday seemed to have faded into an indistinct blur.

It all seemed so long ago now. Her mind flitted back to her life at work in the office at Crawford and Jackson, typing in the office next door to Linda. Meeting Linda for lunch and taking the tube home with her, day after day the same routine. It all seemed so distant, so unreal now. What would life be like, she wondered, when Luke left?

She realised she had been talking for twenty minutes, and quickly rounded up the story. Graham watched her with a mischievous grin.

'That all?' he enquired, one eyebrow raised merrily.

Kate averted her face. 'That's it,' she told him firmly, her eyes fixing on a point just below her hands.

'Ha!' Graham snorted, rapping his nails on the shiny crash helmet which he still held in his hands.

Mrs Scott frowned at Graham. 'Now then, that's enough of that. Kate's told all there is to tell.'

He held up his hands. 'I believe her, I believe her! Thousands wouldn't, but I do, because I'm such a loving soul.'

Mrs Scott sighed. 'Why don't you go and play with your motorbike, dear? You don't seem to be helping much in here.'

Graham shrugged and grinned at Kate. 'Mum, you're about as subtle as a poke in the eye!' He stood up, whistling under his breath. 'Still, I know when

I'm not wanted. I'll go and change the wheel. It could do with a bit of polishing up.'

Kate laughed, feeling relieved. Graham could be very embarrassing at times, but at least he knew when to drop a subject.

Graham shuffled out of the kitchen, taking his crash helmet with him as he walked towards the front door.

'Don't you bring it inside,' Mrs Scott called after him as he stepped out of the front door. 'I won't have that smelly thing in the house!'

Kate sat down on a chair, her head resting in her hands, and stared into space. She knew Luke would leave as soon as he had sorted out everything with her parents. After all, that was the only reason he had come down here with her. She suddenly realised she didn't want him to go.

Even after all he had accused her of, after everything that had been said, she felt a sharp pang of disappointment inside her at the thought of never seeing him again. Why? she asked herself, frowning. Why did her feelings have to be so contradictory and confusing?

The sound of the living room door opening caught her attention, and she turned to look towards the doorway.

Mr Scott stood relaxed and cheerful, watching her. 'I've sorted everything out with Luke. I'll support the story you released to the press.'

Kate smiled warmly. She gave him a little kiss as she passed him to go into the other room. Luke looked up as she entered, his sensual mouth curving into a smile. She sat next to him on the sofa, and for the rest of the afternoon he continued to exert his charm on her family.

How does he do it? she wondered as she watched both her parents fall under his spell. An invitation was extended to him to stay for dinner, but he politely refused. He said he had to go back to the city to speak to his publicity agent.

Kate felt a bitter stab as she heard his words. She knew who his publicity agent was—Lisa Blair. Would he be dining with her instead tonight? she wondered.

All too soon time had passed, and Luke stood up, firmly telling them that he really had to leave. Kate left the room after him, saying she would see him to the door.

She had a strange sense of foreboding, as though she would never see him again. In the darkened hallway, her eyes flickered over his features, trying to imprint them on her memory. As he slid into his coat, she watched with fascination as the powerful muscles rippled, her eyes lowering to his long, long legs. Kate felt a sense of longing overwhelm her. She pushed it away, confused and disturbed at the emotions he was capable of arousing in her.

He turned to look at her. 'How long will you be here for?' he asked quietly.

Kate blinked, her eyes lifting to his face. 'I don't know. Probably until after Christmas. There's no point in going back to work until next Monday. I can imagine the reception I'll get when I do go back there.'

He nodded. 'You'll have Tuesday, Wednesday, and Thursday off too, won't you?'

She smiled brightly, feeling very, very sad for some reason. 'It is Christmas.'

A smile touched the hard mouth. 'You did say you were a secretary, didn't you?'

Kate was puzzled. 'Yes.'

'Who do you work for?' he asked, his head tilted to one side as he watched her.

'Crawford and Jackson, the publishing firm,' she told him with a shrug.

Luke nodded, then buttoned up his coat, pulling the collar up high, and turned to the front door. 'I'll be in touch before you leave,' he told her, his hand on the front door.

Kate felt a tremendous sense of loss as she watched him open the door. She didn't want him to go. She stood, rooted to the spot, frozen in indecision and confusion. She wanted to call him back. But she stood, silent and still.

Luke turned back, moving towards her. A smile curved his mouth, and his blue eyes twinkled. Before she knew what he was going to do, his black head bent towards her, and his hard lips brushed against hers.

Kate stared with wide eyes, her heart immobile for a moment. Then it kicked back into life, but he drew away almost immediately.

'Goodnight, Kate,' he said softly, his voice a husky murmur. Then he was gone, the door was closed, and she was alone in the darkened hallway with nothing but her thoughts and her memories to keep her company.

She felt confused, sad, and very much alone.

CHAPTER SIX

LIFE seemed very quiet after her meeting with Luke, and the days trailed off slowly, the hours ticking by with relentless fatigue. Kate spent her time helping her mother around the house, trying to keep herself busy, her mind occupied.

Whenever she sat down to rest, she would find Luke's face jumping into her mind, his blue eyes glittering at her, disturbing her. She would relive the conversations she had had with him, remember the way he touched her, kissed her. It was at those times that she would get up, determined to stop herself thinking, and find some small task that would cut off all thought.

On Christmas Eve she took Sergeant Humphrey for a walk, feeling the need for some fresh air. The dog pulled frantically at the leash, almost pulling her over on several occasions.

Keyford was situated in a valley, built within the sanctuary of the low hills that surrounded it. Kate took the dog outside the built-up area of the town, up into the hills. Together they clambered along the soft green carpets of grass, Sergeant Humphrey dodging among the dark hedges as he ran ahead of her, pleased to be allowed to run free.

After three-quarters of an hour, she realised it had been a mistake to come out on her own. She found herself walking slowly, huddled in her coat, a

pensive expression on her face. Her thoughts had
turned to Luke once more, and even the chill winter
sunshine couldn't lighten her mood.

She whistled to Sergeant Humphrey and began to
walk briskly back to the house, determined to banish
all thoughts of Luke as soon as she got back within
the safety of her home.

She made a great effort to join in the spirit of
Christmas, wrapping presents with her mother,
adding further decorations to the already laden tree
that sparkled in the middle of the living room. She
laughed with forced gaiety as they consumed hot
mince pies and brandy at midnight. But she went to
bed feeling tired and lonely, and slipped into a dull,
heavy sleep, waking on Christmas morning with a
slight headache.

It was the strangest Christmas she had ever
known. All the excitement of previous years was
gone. Even though Graham clowned around as
usual, Kate found it next to impossible to join in.
Christmas had suddenly lost all its magic for her.

On Boxing Day she woke early, and spent two
hours sitting in the kitchen trying to read a book.
Her mind, however, was set on wandering, and she
gave up in disgust after a while, sitting staring
thoughtfully out of the window instead.

After lunch she sat down to try and concentrate
on a film that was being shown on television. She
had drunk three glasses of wine at lunchtime, in an
attempt to relax her and bring her out of herself, but
it merely marred her already wavering sense of con-
centration.

Graham loped into the room, his long gangly arms

hanging down by his sides. He regarded the television with disgust. 'What's this old garbage?' he enquired.

Kate had to agree with him. The film really wasn't much good, so she picked up the Radio and TV Times and began flicking through them. She shrugged. 'Nothing on the other side,' she told him dully.

Graham scratched his ear with a bony finger. 'Cheerful soul, aren't you?' he observed, his clear brown eyes watching her curiously. 'What's the matter? You fallen in love or something?'

Her head came up at that, and she stared at him for a moment in surprise. Was that what was wrong with her? Then she shook her head. Graham was only teasing her, he hadn't been serious when he had said that. She was becoming fanciful.

Her mind flitted back, once more, to Luke. Life seemed so quiet now, although she knew that she had lived in this way for most of her life. But knowing that didn't help much. Luke had had such a major effect on her life that she found it hard to shake his memory off.

He had said he would come back before she left, but Kate doubted that he would; he was probably just making rash promises. But she couldn't seem to stop herself jumping when the telephone rang, listening out for the sound of his car, wondering where he was and what he was doing.

Graham shambled over to the window. 'Think I'll go and tinker with my bike. She could do with a quick polish.'

Kate stood up too, and wandered over to the

bookcase beside him. She scanned the shelves for a book that might keep her mind away from Luke. Titles leapt out at her, but she wasn't really interested in them.

Graham continued to look out of the window, his eyes gleaming as they rested on his motorbike. Suddenly he whistled, and turned his head slightly to look in Kate's direction.

'Hello,' he said, peering back out of the window. 'Methinks we have visitors.'

Mrs Scott, who had previously been knitting in complete silence as though she were totally alone in the room, lifted her head now, and looked with interest at Graham. 'Visitors?' she echoed, putting down her knitting. 'What visitors?'

Kate moved to the window and looked out, her eyes widening as she saw the sleek black sports car. She drew in her breath as she noticed the woman in the front seat next to Luke. But it wasn't Lisa Blair. In that case, who was it? Her eyes were riveted on Luke's harsh profile, etched clearly in the front of the car.

The sun reflected off the car door as he opened it and got out. The woman stepped out of her side of the car, standing tall and elegant in the chill winter sunshine.

Graham whistled under his breath. 'That is a mean machine,' he observed in awe as Kate threw him an irritated glance.

'You're left over from another era, Graham,' she told him crossly as she continued to stare out of the window.

The woman's hair was black, falling in a smooth

bell around her face, her skin sallow, and her eyes, even from this distance, were a sharp blue.

They began to walk up the path to the front door, and Kate left the room quickly and went into the hallway.

She opened the front door slowly. Luke towered over her, his dazzling blue eyes staring broodingly into hers. The woman by his side watched them with shrewd eyes, her gaze flitting from one to the other, missing nothing in their expressions.

Luke smiled, 'Hello, Kate.'

She swallowed and nodded. 'Hello.' Her voice was nervous as she stared at the woman by his side.

The woman stared back with clever, unwinking blue eyes. Her black hair fell in a smooth curve around her sharp face, her nose turned up at the end above her small, bow-shaped lips, giving her the appearance of a little pixie. She looked at Luke, her thin, dark brows raised in enquiry. 'Aren't you going to introduce us?' she drawled.

Luke shot a wry glance at her, and turned to Kate with a smile. 'Kate, I'd like you to meet my sister Janet. Janet,' he indicated Kate, 'this is Kate.'

Kate's mouth dropped open as she looked first at Luke, then at his sister. She saw the likeness now, the rich dark colour of the hair, the same shrewd eyes.

Janet watched with amusement. 'Catching flies?' A smile pulled at her lips.

Kate almost blushed. Then she saw the dry amusement in Janet's eyes, and smiled at her.

'It's cold out here,' Janet remarked, raising a brow as she began to walk into the hall, watching with amusement as Kate backed, opening the door wider to enable them to pass.

Luke followed his sister into the house, an angry expression on his face. 'Don't be so rude, Janet,' he told her curtly, his voice crisp.

Janet regarded him with irritation. 'Don't be silly, Luke. Kate doesn't mind, do you, dear?' She gave Kate a brusque smile, then turned to Luke before she had a chance to reply. 'See? You're too stuffy, brother dear.'

Kate stifled a smile as she saw the resigned expression creep over Luke's face. He was obviously used to his sister's ways, and Janet obviously knew how to handle him. I wish I did, Kate thought, remembering all the times he had shouted at her, accusing her of things which she hadn't done.

Janet handed Kate her coat with a flourish and moved off into the house. 'Where's the living room?' she asked, poking her head round the door in which Graham and Mrs Scott still sat, waiting expectantly. 'Hello,' Janet said, going into the room. 'Who are you?'

Luke gave a sigh of exasperation and dived in after her. He performed the introductions before anyone had a chance to realise how inquisitive Janet was being.

Janet eyed Graham, her gaze skimming over his appearance. 'Hello,' she said slowly. 'I take it you're the mad motorbike boy.'

Graham looked pleased, his face filling with pride as his eyes twinkled cheekily at her. 'That's me,' he said cheerfully. 'How did you guess?'

Janet raised thin eyebrows at him, her expression

dry. 'I nearly tripped over your wretched machine as I was coming up the path,' she told him, and smiled as she finished speaking.

Mrs Scott disappeared to make some tea and cakes, a maternal glint in her eye as she dusted her pinny happily. Kate searched her mind for something to say. She had no idea why Luke had brought his sister down here on Boxing Day. He must have a reason, she thought with a frown, he wouldn't just turn up on the doorstep to make a social call.

She finally decided on polite, neutral conversation. She cleared her throat and asked, 'Did you have a nice Christmas?'

Luke watched her with sardonic eyes. 'Yes, thank you,' he said in an amused tone, 'we had a very good Christmas.'

Janet looked at her brother with a dry expression. 'You may have done, but then you didn't have to put up with yourself for three days,' she told him with a smile.

Graham loped across the room, picking up his crash helmet as he did so. He slid into his jacket and waved a bony hand at them all, saying, 'I'm going round to see my friends. Have fun!'

Kate felt even more isolated and uncomfortable after Graham had left. She had no idea of what to say to Luke and Janet. She had been thinking of Luke ever since he had left a few days previously, and now that he was here, in front of her, her mind seemed to have dried up.

Janet was quick to notice this. She smiled at Kate, raising her thin, dark brows. 'Don't look so worried! I haven't come down here to form part of the

Spanish Inquisition. I know my brother is a bully, but I'm not.'

Luke gave her an offended look. 'I'm not a bully,' he protested.

'Don't tell lies,' Janet said with mock severity, 'or your nose will grow.'

Kate stifled another smile as she watched Luke lean back in his seat and fold his arms with a sigh of resignation. He looked across at her and winked at her, which did decidedly strange things to Kate's heartbeat. She pulled herself together, averting her gaze from his face, frightened of the feelings which were beginning to come rushing back at her like an out-of-control steam train.

Kate leaned forward in her seat, thinking of the right words with which to phrase her question. She wanted to know exactly why they were here, but she didn't want to sound rude. After all, they could be merely visiting her, paying a social call, in which case they would no doubt be offended if Kate asked why they were here.

Janet, however, was quick to read the expression on her face. 'You want to know why we're here?' she drawled, her mouth lifting at one corner.

Kate smiled grudgingly. 'Well, I did wonder,' she admitted. 'I didn't expect to see Luke until the day I left.' She glanced at him to see how he reacted to this. Perhaps that remark had sounded presumptuous or too expectant. But she was worrying for nothing; Luke smiled at her.

Janet fixed Kate with her sharp blue eyes and said blandly, 'I've come to offer you a job.'

Kate's brows rose unconsciously. Whatever she

had been expecting, it had certainly not been that. 'What sort of job?' she asked with a frown.

'Secretarial,' Janet replied briskly. 'I need someone to help me organise my work. I'm writing a book, and at the moment I'm still gathering material for it. The first two chapters are done, but there's a hell of a lot of stuff on the tapes that needs unravelling.'

Kate frowned again, her head tilted to one side as she listened. 'What sort of book is it?'

Janet smiled crookedly, her eyes sliding to Luke. 'It's the official biography of someone not a million miles from here.'

Kate's eyes widened. She looked at Luke, who was listening to this exchange with a wry expression on his face. His gaze caught Kate's and held it, and his mouth curved in a smile. 'Janet's been working on it for six months,' he told her, his voice deep and crisp. 'I got so fed up with the press and the magazines writing all that rubbish about me that I decided to get the truth down, clear up a few old myths.'

Kate's interest was thoroughly aroused by now. She had been intrigued by the idea of working for an author, knowing that the work would be both satisfying and enjoyable. But biographies had always fascinated her, because people's lives were always woven with such intricate and fascinating detail.

'What would the work entail?' she asked, leaning forward with interest as she spoke.

'Well,' Janet ran a hand through her glossy black hair, smoothing the fringe down over her forehead with her palm, 'Luke's been jabbering endlessly into the tape recorder about his life and work, etc, etc.

What has to be done is to put the tapes in order, clear up the loose ends and get it down on paper,' she paused, her sharp blue eyes boring into Kate's. 'It'll be hard work. I don't put up with people lying around all day doing nothing. I'll expect you to work as hard as I do.'

Kate returned her gaze steadily. 'I'm not afraid of hard work.'

'No,' Janet said, nodding slowly, 'I'm sure you're not.'

Luke stood up, his long legs uncoiling gracefully. He shoved his hands into his pockets and walked over to stand by the window. 'It'll involve some travelling,' he told Kate, turning his black head to look at her.

Kate frowned. 'Where to?'

'New York.' Janet dropped the bombshell with great aplomb. Her voice was brisk, but her shrewd gaze was fixed firmly on Kate as she watched her for signs of shock. 'We have to follow him over there next month.'

Luke walked back slowly, standing over Kate, watching as the amazed expression on her face slowly receded. 'I have to go over there for some recording and interviews. It'll make good material for the book,' he glanced at his sister, 'or so I'm told.'

Janet gave him a sweet smile. 'That's right, sweetie-pie,' she told him in a voice like melted honey. 'Not many people know what it's like inside a recording studio. I'm sure a lot of people would be very interested to read a little on the subject.'

Kate had to agree. She had never seen inside a studio, except perhaps the unrealistic glimpses one gained through television. It would unquestionably make good material for the book.

She looked at Luke with a frown. 'Why have you asked me to work for your sister?' It had been troubling her all along, ever since Janet had announced so blandly that that was why they were here. There were so many good secretaries they could pick—why her?

Janet raised her eyebrows. 'You're not going to be working for him, dear. I'm writing the book—I'm the one who needs a secretary.'

Luke glanced at his sister. Then he looked back at Kate, his eyes glinting between thick black lashes. 'I checked with Crawford and Jackson before Christmas, and they gave me the name of the company you worked for before you joined them. You come highly recommended.'

Kate frowned. How did he know he could trust her? He had made it plain on Saturday that he thought she was behind the whole mess they had been in last week. Why had his attitude changed so vastly in so short a space of time?

'Well?' Janet's brisk voice broke into her thoughts. 'What do you say? Do you want the job?'

Kate thought for a moment. She was immensely interested in what she would be doing. Anyone with half a brain would be interested, she thought with a smile, especially as a trip to New York went hand in hand with the job. She would be a fool to turn it down.

She made her decision in a split second. 'Yes,' she looked at Janet, 'I'll come and work for you,' and watched as Janet's small, bow-shaped mouth curved in triumph.

'Good,' she said, standing up. 'That's settled, then. Have you got a passport?' At Kate's nod she continued, 'I'll organise a visa for you as soon as possible. Luke will attend to the other details, won't you, dear?' She grinned at her brother.

Luke nodded and looked down at Kate. 'How soon do you think you can start?'

She shrugged, spreading her hands before her. 'I'll have to phone my former boss...Monday?'

'Sounds good,' Janet said briskly, smoothing a hand over the smooth bell of her black hair. 'Now, if you'll excuse me, I'll go and see whether Kate's mother needs a hand in the kitchen.' She walked to the door and left the room with a backward smile.

Very subtle, thought Kate, staring at her feet uncomfortably, unable to look Luke in the eye. She felt very dazed by the suddenness of the offer of this job. She had had to decide so quickly that she hadn't had time to consider carefully all the points involved. What would she do about her flat? Where in London would she be working? What would she do about Linda? So many questions, and, as usual, so few answers.

She looked up slowly as she became aware that Luke was watching her, his tall, powerful body blocking her view.

'Second thoughts?' he queried.

Kate shook her head, frowning. 'No, I'm looking forward to beginning my new job. I'm just trying to take it all in, that's all,' she smiled slightly, 'You must admit it's come as rather a surprise to me!'

He nodded. 'Janet has a way of pouncing on

people like that. She can be a bit overpowering at times,' he agreed with a trace of amusement in the deep, rich tones.

'It isn't that,' she told him directly, 'I was just trying to figure out why I was offered the job in the first place.'

Luke's lashes flickered slightly, and he watched her from beneath heavy lids. His hard mouth was pursed as he looked at her thoughtfully for a second, then he reached out a hand, his lean brown fingers closing over her wrist. He pulled her gently over to the sofa and sat down next to her, his long legs stretched lazily before him.

Kate felt rather bewildered. The change in his attitude towards her was so great. She watched him suspiciously out of the corner of her eye, wishing she could walk inside his head and see what he was thinking.

'Why did you pick me to be your sister's secretary?' she asked him quietly.

He sighed, raking a hand through his thick black hair. He looked across at her, his eyes glinting with the reflection from the leaping flames of the log fire opposite them.

'You wouldn't have been considered for the job if you hadn't been capable of doing it,' he told her firmly. 'I found out from your employers that you were hard-working and efficient, and that paved the way for you.'

Kate tilted her head to one side. 'But you made it plain on Saturday that you thought I was responsible for the story in the papers,' she pointed out. 'What makes you think you can trust me to work for your sister?'

Perhaps now she would get some answers. She wondered, once again, what his motive was. It seemed so strange that he should have changed this much.

He grimaced, spreading his hands in front of him and looking down at them. 'On Saturday I was very angry, so I blamed the nearest person.'

Kate looked at him as he turned back to face her, and a glint of mischief entered her eyes.

'And?' she pressed, trying to keep the smile out of her voice.

'And,' he said slowly, 'I've had time to reconsider. I've thought it over.'

Kate leaned forward, her green eyes alight with amusement. She knew he was on the threshold of apologising to her for his behaviour on Saturday, and she wasn't going to let him off without hearing him say it.

She caught and held his gaze, raising her brows in silent expectation as she tilted her head to one side.

Luke shrugged, looking uncomfortable. 'I was wrong about you. I misjudged you.'

Kate suppressed the smile that was hovering around her lips. 'And?' she pressed, her voice as soft as silk.

A scowl crossed Luke's face and he drew in his breath slowly. 'And I owe you an apology,' he muttered.

Kate raised her brows once more, watching him impishly. She would make him apologise if it killed her!

Luke looked at her, his black brows drawn together in a frown over the top of his autocratic nose.

Kate laughed, her eyes twinkling with amusement. 'Apology accepted!' she said brightly.

Luke frowned, and his eyes narrowed. He scowled. Then a smile tugged at the corners of his hard mouth, and his long, sinewy fingers reached out to capture her wrist, pulling her towards him.

'You little minx,' he said in a rich, deep, amused voice as he lay back against the soft cushions, pulling her down with him.

Kate couldn't help herself as she fell into his arms, laughing, the thick swathe of her glossy black hair falling over her eyes and brushing his cheek. His face was so close to hers, his breath fanning her cheek as he laughed softly. She looked up into his eyes.

The laughter stopped, and their eyes met and held. She heard his sharp intake of breath, saw the deep glitter in his eyes. His mouth brushed tentatively against hers, making her pulse begin to thud, her heartbeat increase. She lay against him, her soft warm body submissive in his arms, feeling every muscle in his body.

His hot mouth moved seductively against hers, his tongue flicking against her lips. Her arms went around his neck to entangle her fingers in his thick hair.

The kiss deepened, becoming more intense, and Kate felt a sweet rush of hot pleasure flood through her. His hand moved on her back, his long fingers stroking her, bringing her closer, lying against him.

His hand slid sensuously down her back, sending sharp stabs of sexual excitement through her, heightened when his long fingers began to stroke the flat plains of her stomach. Kate groaned from deep in the back of her throat.

Luke's breathing accelerated as he left her mouth to run his lips along her cheek. His arms tightened around her as she moved softly against him. His mouth moved back to hers, hot and demanding as it moved harder against hers, passion flaming between them, and his hand stroked her neck with experienced fingers.

His mouth left hers, moving to kiss the side of her throat, and Kate moaned, feeling tingles rushing up and down her body from her head right down to her toes. Her hands tangled tighter in his hair, pulling him closer, delighting in the feel of his mouth against her neck.

His tongue snaked out across her throat, and Kate shuddered with pleasure, drawing in her breath sharply, losing all thought and responsibility as his mouth moved up towards her ear. He nibbled at the sensitive lobe, his strong white teeth gentle and exciting.

'I'm going to enjoy our working holiday,' he murmured in husky tones against her ear, his tongue licking her delicate skin. 'You're so beautiful, Kate.'

Kate stiffened. In that moment he had lost her. The feelings he had evoked in her disappeared, leaving a cold, hard knot inside her stomach. She lay rigid beneath him for a second, then moved her hands, pushing at his hard chest.

He raised his head, his eyes black in the centre of the dazzling blue. His brows were drawn together in a frown as he looked down blankly at her. 'What's wrong, darling?' he murmured huskily.

Her lips tightened. Darling? She'd give him darling, the conniving devil! 'I've changed my mind,' she said, her voice trembling with anger. 'I'm not taking the job.'

His frown deepened. 'Why not?'

She sat up, pushing him away from her with shaking hands. 'If you think,' she said between dry lips, 'that I'm coming to New York as your plaything, then you're sorely mistaken!'

'What the hell are you talking about?' he demanded.

'You know what I'm talking about!' she snapped back, then bit her lip, trying to control her anger, trying to hide from the shame building up inside her. Her response to his kiss had been stupid, but she'd be damned if she'd pay for it by becoming his mistress in America!

She looked back at him, her green eyes filled with angry sparks. 'I will not become your mistress for you to pass the time with in the States!'

His teeth snapped together like a steel trap. 'Did I ask you to?'

'In so many words, yes,' she told him bitterly.

Luke raked a hand through his hair. His face was harsh and angry, his mouth compressed into a firm line. The skin across his cheekbones was taut, showing the white of his bones.

'You read too damned much into a kiss,' he muttered, standing up and walking over to the window with his hands pushed into his pockets.

Kate sat where she was, feeling the trembling recede. She knew she had acted rather late, but she was glad she had acted. It was better to know where she stood. Thank God she hadn't waited until she was hundreds of miles from England to find out what his real intentions were!

Luke was staring out of the window. He turned his black head slightly to look at her. 'I won't lay another finger on you,' he said abruptly, his voice hard and cold as ice.

She shook her head. 'That makes no difference.'

He swore under his breath. 'Take the blasted job! I can promise you you'll have no trouble from me. I'm not in the habit of forcing women to sleep with me.'

She looked up. 'How can I be sure?' Her voice was quiet, almost a whisper.

His mouth hardened. 'Oh, you can be sure all right,' he said grimly, 'I'll keep well away from you.'

Kate began to say something, but at that moment Janet came into the room with the tea. She stopped in the centre of the room, her sharp blue eyes going from Luke to Kate and back again. One could almost hear her sniffing the atmosphere like a bloodhound.

Kate suddenly felt a rush of uncertainty. She desperately wanted to take the job. Not only did she want to work with Janet, help her to put the book together, but she wanted something else. She wanted to be with Luke. She didn't want him to go away and never come back again.

She bit her lip, frightened to speak up. What would Luke think of her if she retracted now and agreed to go to New York? It would almost be as though she had handed herself to him on a silver platter. But she couldn't bear the thought of never seeing him again. At least if she was working with his sister, she would come into some kind of contact with him.

Janet's brows were raised in enquiry. 'Well?' she asked, looking at Luke, her smooth black hair swinging into place as she turned.

'She's going to take the job,' Luke said harshly, his hard blue eyes daring Kate to contradict him. 'We leave for New York at the end of January.'

CHAPTER SEVEN

KATE gazed out of the smoked glass window of the limousine in rapt fascination. New York City was in the grip of a bitter, icy winter, and pulsating with life all around her. The sound of traffic echoed in the cold afternoon, horns blowing loudly, brakes squealing, irate drivers swearing and shouting as the cars pulled jerkily through the thick stream of traffic.

People darted in and out of the traffic, crossing from one side of the wide main road to the other. The people who made their frantic way along the sidewalks were dressed in thick winter coats, scarves wrapped tightly around their necks. They walked briskly, watching their breath steam in front of them, their collars up, their hands pushed deep into their pockets.

The buildings were tall, reaching higher than she could ever have imagined, making the city seem open and large and free. Great concrete and glass structures towered wherever the eye looked, reaching up towards the cloudy white sky.

Since stepping off the plane in top secrecy at Kennedy Airport, Kate had found her admiration of New York increasing minute by minute. It was all so vast, so far beyond her imagination. The airport had stretched welcomingly before her, a vast glass and metal building which beckoned to her, offering warmth and comfort across the freezing tarmac.

Janet shifted in the seat beside her. 'I'll never complain about English weather again,' she remarked drily, peering out of the window at the cold, fast-moving streets.

Luke laughed softly. 'I'll remember that,' he promised, 'next time we're in England!'

Kate glanced across at them with a slight smile. Luke was leaning back against the plush seat of the car, a relaxed look on his face. The chauffeur turned smoothly to the left, and Luke turned to look at Kate. His eyes were hooded, looking at her through his thick black lashes.

Kate smiled tentatively, but Luke's face remained impassive, and he turned away from her. Kate looked down at her hands, feeling foolish. Ever since she had started working for Janet, he had consistently treated her with cool, offhand formality.

She sighed, looking back out of the window. She had given her notice in to Crawford and Jackson, receiving raised eyebrows and knowing smiles as she did so. She had been glad to leave, quite frankly. She knew she wouldn't have been able to cope with working in an atmosphere like that. After the story in the papers, her life had changed in so many major ways, least of all her job.

She had eventually decided to give up her flat. Linda had not been pleased. She had shrieked, pleaded, sulked and snarled at Kate. But, in the end, Linda had realised that Kate was not going to carry on living with her. It hadn't been personal, Kate had explained, merely necessary and practical. She could hardly live in London when she was working in Kent for a month, followed quickly by a trip to New York and a return to London.

Kate's eyes swept unseeingly over the outside world. No doubt Linda would have found a new flatmate by the time she returned from New York. It was easy to find people to live with in London— flats were so scarce. The problem was making sure they were the right kind of people. One could never tell on first impressions exactly what a person might get up to in their spare time. Linda wouldn't, surely, want to install a troublemaker in her home.

Kate shrugged her thoughts aside. She couldn't spend the rest of her life worrying over Linda. She had to look after herself, although Kate would always be ready to lend her a helping hand.

She looked out of the window, feeling an upsurge of excitement. She desperately wanted to get out and walk among the huge skyscrapers, along the wide sidewalks, breathing in the life and vibrations of New York. It was all so exciting and new to her. She had never dreamed that a city could inspire such breathless excitement in her.

New York City was dynamic, alive, burning with life and movement.

The limousine pulled up smoothly outside the doors of a beautiful hotel. On the corner of Fifth Avenue, it offered a superb view of Central Park, just over the street from the hotel. Kate looked up as the hotel doorman panted down the steps at break-neck speed.

Luke walked gracefully up the hotel steps, his black cashmere overcoat pulled up at the collar to protect his neck from the icy wind. Janet and Kate walked by his side into the hotel.

Kate felt the warmth of the interior wrap itself around her as she noticed a man coming forwards to greet Luke.

'Luke!' The man's blond hair brushed the tip of his collar, falling in layered waves, glimmering in the light from the foyer ceiling. His face was bony, open and friendly, with a slightly boyish look about it, and the warm brown eyes danced with cheerfulness as he shook Luke's hand with verve.

Luke smiled, his face relaxed as he greeted the man. 'Hello, Steve. Good to be back in New York.'

Kate judged the man called Steve to be in his early thirties. He was very tall, and very slim, dressed in black trousers and a white jacket with a crisp white shirt, emphasising how very slim he was.

'Janet!' Steve gave her a big smile, taking her hand and shaking it with as much verve as he had Luke's. 'How are you doing?'

Janet gave a mock grimace. 'Not so good. I'm cold and I'm tired,' she told him, smiling wryly.

Steve nodded his head in agreement, his lips pulling down slightly. 'Yeah,' he agreed solemnly, 'we've been having a bad winter this year.' His gaze swivelled to Kate, skimming over her with appreciation as his face brightened with cheer. 'Hello,' he said with emphasis.

Luke's face was enigmatic as he too turned towards Kate. 'This is Kate Scott, Janet's secretary. Kate, this is Steve Beck, a director of M.D.C. Records.'

Steve extended a smooth, tanned hand, his grip firm and friendly. 'Pleased to meet you, Kate,' he said in a heavy New York accent. 'Anything I can do for you while you're in my city, just let me know—I'll be right over.'

Janet and Kate laughed. Luke didn't. His face was controlled as he watched the exchange.

Janet spotted this and gave her brother a wry little smile. 'She might need protection if this sort of reaction carries on everywhere we go!'

Steve laughed. 'I'll be glad to protect you, anytime. Nobody knows Noo Yawk as good as I do, and I'll be happy to be your bodyguard while you're here,' he told Kate in a heavily exaggerated New York drawl.

Kate smiled at him with genuine warmth. She liked Steve Beck, she decided. He was friendly and amusing, if a little brash, and his eyes were sincere. He was only trying to make her feel welcome—she knew enough about men to know that he wasn't seriously flirting with her.

Luke was watching her with a hard expression on his face. 'Would you like to settle into your room first,' he asked in a crisp, slightly curt voice, 'or would you rather have a drink in the bar before you go up?'

Kate shrugged. She was feeling very tired physically, but her mind was very much alive. It was funny how travelling tired one out, she thought, when all one did was sit still for hours on end.

Janet answered Luke. 'I'd like go up, if you don't mind,' she told her brother in a slightly weary voice. 'I'm tired and I want to take a shower before I get some sleep.'

Luke nodded. 'Fair enough.' He looked at Kate,

one jet-black eyebrow raised. 'And you?' he enquired in a distant but polite voice.

'Yes, I think I'll go on up too. I'm quite tired after all that travelling.' She kept her voice as deliberately blank as his had been.

'Right.' Luke glanced at his watch, and Kate's eyes strayed to his wrist, noting the way the black hairs grew all around the gold watch, peeping out from beneath his black overcoat. She looked away. Luke studied her with cold eyes. 'I'll stay down here for a while. I have some business to discuss with Steve. It's four o'clock now.' He looked at both her and Janet. 'Shall we say seven-thirty for dinner?'

Kate nodded and, after saying goodbye to Steve, she and Janet made their way up to their rooms, following the two porters who carried their luggage.

'I hope Luke gets some rest before dinner,' Janet remarked idly as they came out of the lift on the fifteenth floor. 'He's been in a filthy temper all day, and it's getting worse by the hour.'

Kate smiled as they walked down the corridor. Luke had been in a perpetual bad mood ever since she had met him.

Kate turned to Janet as the porter stopped outside her room and opened the door, taking the luggage in. 'Is there any work you wanted to do before tonight? If there is, I can always fit it in now, while you go and rest.'

Janet shook her head wryly. 'Not today, old chum,' she told her, her black hair swinging from side to side, 'I'm going to rest my poor old brain for a few hours.'

Kate smiled. 'Okay. I'll see you at dinner, then,'

and she moved just inside the door.

'Right-oh,' said Janet. 'And don't forget to get some sleep. Jet lag is pretty nasty, and you won't recover from it unless you catch a few hours now.'

Janet went off down the corridor, following the porter, and Kate closed her own door after giving the porter a tip.

She walked over to the window, looking down on to the main street below. New York beckoned to her noisily. Cars passed on the road below her, looking small and remote from the height of her room on the fifteenth floor.

The noise of the city below and around her was almost like music. She leant against the window with a smile, feeling the excitement well up once more, wishing she was out there among the noise, the life, the energy.

A wave of sadness washed over her, and a frown of pain marred her forehead. What good was it, being in this magical city, breathing in the life of the town, when she had nobody to share it with?

She walked over to her bed and began to unpack slowly, her thoughts on Luke, a brooding expression on her face.

Kate sat in front of the dressing table mirror. She brushed her long, silky black hair, allowing it to fall in unruly curls around her shoulders. It was still wet from her shower, and smelt clean and fresh. She wore only a hint of make-up, a touch of mascara, her lips highlighted with lip-gloss.

She smoothed the flame-red dress over her hips, eyeing her reflection critically. Her slender figure was sensuous but discreet in the dress.

She stifled a yawn as she glanced at her watch. It was gone half-past seven, and she was late. She had meant to explore the city before dinner, but as soon as she had closed her eyes, she had fallen asleep.

A knock on the door brought her head up, a frown marring her brow. She crossed the room and opened the door, peering round it to see who was there.

'Oh, it's you,' she said, opening the door wider.

Luke raised one jet-black brow. 'I came to see what had happened to you,' he told her as he walked lazily into the room. 'I should have realised you were spending hours painting your face.'

Kate compressed her lips irritably. 'I wasn't painting my face.' She lifted her face to show him. 'See? I hardly have any make-up on at all.'

Luke looked closely at her. 'So you haven't,' he murmured. 'Good girl. You don't need it anyway.'

Kate picked her bag up from the table and sifted through it, checking for her key. Her hand closed over the long black plastic key tag. She closed the bag and went over to the bedside table to pick up her silver necklace.

Luke walked up behind her, his long legs moving as quietly and deceptively as a panther's.

'Allow me,' he murmured, his voice dark and lazy as he deftly took the necklace from her hands. His long brown hands closed over her shoulders, and he gently turned her to face the mirror. He stood behind her, looking at her reflection in the mirror, and Kate felt her face grow heated. His cool fingers moved the necklace around her neck, behind her newly washed hair.

His dazzling blue eyes held hers in the mirror, looking over her shoulder as he fastened the clasp. Kate stared back at him, her heart beginning to move slightly faster inside her. Her eyes were large and startled as she found herself unable to tear them from his.

Luke's black head bent slowly, his eyes still riveted on hers. He pressed his mouth against her neck and she felt a shiver run through her body.

There was a little silence. His eyes flickered down over the length of her body with a deeply sensual movement. They rested on her breasts, high and firm beneath the flame red silk, and she could almost feel the heat of his gaze searing her flesh.

His eyes moved slowly back up to her face, looking deep into her wide, startled eyes. 'You're beautiful,' he murmured in her ear, his hot mouth moving down to her throat, his hands firm on her shoulders.

Kate swallowed nervously. Luke's change in attitude towards her was confusing. He had been curt and abrupt with her since she had started working for Janet. Now he was in her hotel room, kissing her. A thought flashed through her mind.

He still wanted her to become his mistress while they were here. Her back stiffened, her neck going rigid. Luke stopped kissing her neck, his black head lifting to look at her with narrowed eyes.

She moved away from him. 'Shall we go down?' she asked in a clear voice, hoping she betrayed no hint of the nervousness she felt.

Luke's face took on an enigmatic, controlled look, and his eyes became hidden behind hooded lids. He tilted his black head to one side.

'Why not?' he said coolly, moving towards the door.

They walked to the lift in an uneasy silence. Kate's mind ticked over, rapidly as she walked beside him. All the time she had been in England, he had been distant, as though he didn't give a damn whether she was alive or not. Now he was changing his tack, and trying to seduce her.

Her lips tightened. If he thought she was going to fall into his arms without a murmur, he had another think coming! She stood beside him in the lift, feeling the nervousness subside, being replaced with indignation at his attitude. Luke thought he was irresistible, did he? Well, she would just have to try and resist him.

Luke caught her eye as they walked out of the lift, and she looked straight through him, before flicking her eyes contemptuously away.

You're wasting your precious time on me, she thought angrily, holding her back rigid as they walked towards the bar. Luke's hand was on her arm, his strong fingers curling possessively on her flesh.

Steve and Janet were already seated at a table with their drinks, and Steve looked up cheerfully as Luke and Kate went towards them.

'Hello, we wondered if you were still alive up there,' he said.

Kate smiled. 'Sorry, I fell asleep as soon as I'd unpacked. I didn't wake up till half an hour ago.'

She sat down while Luke ordered their drinks from a passing waiter.

Janet threw her a dry smile, one dark brow lifted.

'I was just about to come after you myself. We sent Luke up ten minutes ago.'

Kate felt herself redden against her will as she encountered Janet's sharp blue eyes. 'He was waiting while I finished doing my make-up,' she said in as calm a voice as possible.

Janet smiled disbelievingly. 'Well, it's a good job you appeared when you did, or we would have been like the Gotham cheeses.'

Kate was thankful that she didn't pursue the matter further. They sat in the bar talking for twenty minutes, before the waiter informed them in a lazy Southern drawl that their table was ready.

Dinner passed smoothly on the whole. The food was beautifully prepared and served. But Kate was amazed at the sheer size of the portions. She stared at her overflowing plate in dismay.

Steve caught her expression and grinned. 'Too much?'

Kate nodded dumbly. She would never eat all of it. It was like trying to eat Mount Everest!

'Don't worry about it,' Steve told her, his accent an exaggerated drawl. 'Some people can, some people can't.'

Kate stared at him. 'Do you mean there are some people who can actually eat something this size?' she asked in awe.

Steve laughed, his eyes twinkling. 'Sure they can. In the States you're either very fat or very thin.'

Kate raised a disbelieving eyebrow. Then she looked at his plate pointedly. 'Which one are you?'

Steve gave her an offended look, then laughed, and launched into a conversation about American eating habits. Kate found him very amusing, his warm brown eyes friendly and sincere. She liked people with honest faces, and Steve certainly had an honest face.

She was constantly aware of Luke beside her. From time to time she would glance at him through her lashes to find him watching her steadily, his eyes hooded and unreadable. Every time she looked at him, she would feel the tension seep into her, until she was taut as a bowstring.

She stared morosely into her wine glass. Luke was the only man who affected her this way. Even when she had been working at Janet's London house, she had seemed to be on tenterhooks the minute Luke arrived; her back stiffening, her heartbeat stepping up the pace, her nerves jangling.

She slid a glance at Luke. He was still watching her in that unnerving fashion. His hard mouth was straight and firm, with blatant sexuality in his full lower lip.

His eyes opened slightly from their hooded position and she caught the full brilliance of the deep, vivid blue. She turned her head away and jerkily picked up her wine glass, sipping the cool liquid.

'How do you like my city?' Steve asked as they were drinking coffee.

Kate smiled. 'I love it,' she told him sincerely, 'I can't wait to get out and see it properly.'

Steve leaned forward and wagged a thin finger at her. 'You don't *see* a city like New York,' he told her. 'You experience it.'

Kate had to agree with him. He was exactly like the city in which he lived; burning with vitality and life. He was also a born flirt, she decided with a smile.

'Okay,' she said in an amused voice, 'I can't wait to get out and experience New York City.'

Steve laughed, and patted her hand. 'That's the idea!'

Kate leaned back in her seat. She glanced at Luke. His eyes glittered ominously between thick black lashes and his face was harsh as he studied her.

Kate looked away hurriedly. She didn't like the look on his face.

Janet yawned delicately, her fine-boned hand shielding her small mouth. 'God, I'm tired,' she said, stretching her arms out behind her. 'I only managed to snatch a couple of hours this afternoon.'

'Jet-lag,' Steve told her. 'You'll be okay in the morning.'

'Mmm,' Janet agreed resignedly, her mouth compressed in a slim line. 'All the same, I think I'll go on up now, if you don't mind.'

Luke shook his head. 'Not at all,' he said in a dark, lazy voice, glancing across at Steve. 'In fact I think it would be a good idea if we all went up. We've a lot to get done tomorrow.'

Steve shrugged, getting slowly to his feet. 'Okay.' He signalled the waiter in order to sign the bill. 'I'll see you all in the morning at the studio.'

Steve stayed in the restaurant while they said goodnight and went out into the foyer. Janet leaned against the wall in the lift.

'I hate travelling,' she complained to Luke.

Luke looked down at her with a slight smile. 'You also hate having nothing to complain about,' he told her with amusement.

Janet looked at Kate and rolled her eyes heavenwards, and Kate suppressed a smile. The lift doors opened with a muted, luxurious sound and they stepped out.

Janet began searching her bag for her room key. 'Stupid things, keys,' she grumbled, 'you can never find them when you want them.'

Luke eyed her drily. 'Perhaps if you didn't have so much rubbish in your bag, you'd find things a lot quicker.'

Janet pulled out the key, holding it by the long black plastic tag. 'Success!' she grinned, waving it in the air.

They stopped outside Kate's room. Kate took her own key out and began to unlock the door.

' 'Night, Kate,' said Janet with a yawn, her eyes almost closing.

Luke stood in the open doorway as Kate prepared to go in. He thrust his hands into his pockets, his legs apart, and looked at his sister.

'I want to have a word with Kate about tomorrow,' he said casually. 'You go to bed, I'll see you in the morning.'

Kate blushed as she watched the fatigue slowly recede from Janet's face. Her sharp blue eyes fastened on Kate, then flicked back to Luke, a smile on her small mouth.

'I see,' she drawled slowly, one dark brow raised, as her eyes flicked back again to Kate. She started to walk down the corridor. 'Pleasant dreams,' she said drily as she went away.

Kate blushed furiously and glared at Luke. He

had deliberately given Janet the wrong impression. He might just as well have pinned a large notice around her neck!

Luke's brows shot up as he encountered Kate's hostile look, then he inclined his head. 'Shall we go in?'

Kate compressed her lips. 'No, we shall not,' she said, holding the door half-closed to prevent his entrance. 'You can say whatever you want to say out here.'

Luke's mouth twisted into a smile. 'I wouldn't want to wake any of the guests,' he murmured.

'Why should you wake them?' she asked sweetly. 'Were you planning on having a loud conversation?'

Luke shrugged, and moved his foot just inside the room, preventing her from closing the door on him. Kate's fingers tightened on the handle, and she braced herself for any sudden movement from him.

She looked pointedly at his foot, but he deliberately ignored her. She sighed. 'Would you mind being as quick as possible? I really am quite tired, and we do have to be up early.'

'Very well,' he said, his face losing it's smile. 'It's quite simple. You're not to tour the city with Steve Beck.'

Kate frowned, looking at him with a puzzled expression. 'I'm sorry, I don't exactly get your drift.'

'Don't you?' he drawled, leaning casually against the door frame. 'You don't remember asking Steve to take you around New York while we were eating dinner?'

Kate hesitated before replying. Her mind flashed back over all the snippets of conversation she could remember from dinner. She shook her head. 'No, I don't remember anything like that.'

'You hesitated rather too long,' Luke told her coolly, his eyes flickering over her face. 'I'd always believed you to be a more accomplished liar.'

She pursed her lips, trying to think up a suitable reply. She watched angrily as a slow smile curved his sensuous lips. His eyes glittered between thick lashes as he nodded his black head slowly.

'You're ready to admit it now?' he queried, leaning forward.

Her hand gripped the door handle as though it was a life-support. 'I admit nothing,' she snapped. 'I don't know where you got the idea from. I didn't ask Steve to show me around the city, and I can only assume that your imagination is working overtime as usual.'

His eyes narrowed slightly, glinting through his half-closed lids like a tiger's watching his prey. 'Are you telling me I imagined it?' he asked very softly.

Kate shivered at the danger she saw in his face. She swallowed nervously before replying. She didn't want to set a match underneath him by being rude; she had a feeling he would explode any minute. His soft voice and slow smile hid nothing.

'You must have overheard something I said and misunderstood the actual meaning,' she said carefully.

Luke shook his black head. 'I think not.' The words were spoken so softly, so precisely, that Kate felt even more nervous, and began to back imperceptibly.

'Would you tell me exactly what you heard me

say?' she asked hopefully.

Luke regarded her steadily. 'You know damned well what you said. I'm not going to discuss it any further. Just do as I say, hmm?' He moved softly forwards until he towered over her.

Her eyes were level with his powerfully muscled chest. She slowly raised her eyes to his hard, tanned face, and shrank visibly from the danger she saw there.

'Stay away from Beck,' he ordered in a deep, controlled voice, 'or I'll break your beautiful neck.'

Kate shuddered, staring transfixed at him. His face was close to hers, his powerful body blocking the doorway. She couldn't speak; she had a feeling her vocal chords wouldn't work.

'And stay off the streets of New York,' he continued, in the same soft, dangerous voice, 'unless you want to get mugged or raped, or both.'

She watched as he slowly moved off down the corridor like a graceful jungle animal; wild, untamed and sensuous.

His hotel room door closed behind him and Kate shut her own door with a weary sigh. She walked over to the bathroom and stood looking blankly at her reflection.

What on earth had made him so angry? She could understand his worries about the rather dubious safety of the streets of New York. But surely if she was with someone, it would be safer. People only got attacked if they were on their own, she thought.

A frown marred her brow. She couldn't see where he had got the idea from about her asking Steve for a guided tour of the city. It was so incredible. In the first place, she would never, under any circumstances, ask a man out. In the second place, she hardly knew Steve Beck.

She shook her head and went back into the bedroom, getting undressed quickly and sliding between the cool sheets with a sigh.

She really was quite tired, she decided, wriggling her toes to warm them up slightly. In the morning they would go to the studios and she would have a chance to see more of the city by car. She yawned gently, and snuggled up to the pillow, falling asleep within minutes.

CHAPTER EIGHT

THEY had been in the control room of the recording studio for four hours. It was three o'clock in the afternoon and Kate was becoming restless. Luke had been working on the same song for all of the four hours. He had discussed the musical arrangement, the backing, the way the tracks were laid down—in fact, he had discussed everything about the song with Steve and other sound engineers. He had also been singing it over and over again, trying to get it absolutely perfect.

Kate looked through the glass panel in front of them. Luke stood in the studio, hands on his slim hips, his long legs apart, his black head bent as he listened thoughtfully to the music being played back. He wore a pair of headphones around his head, making his thick black hair push out at the front.

Steve sat in the centre of the vast control panel, his face intense as he listened to the song. He stopped the tape and leaned forward, pressing the red microphone button on the deck.

'Did you hear it, Luke?' he asked, speaking into the microphone in front of him.

'The end of that verse?' Luke's dark voice boomed back over the loud speaker system as he spoke into the microphone in front of him.

Steve nodded calmly. 'Yeah, I don't think you have quite the right inflection when the verse ends.'

He paused, his lips pursed as he looked at the panel in front of him. 'Could you try going up rather than holding her steady?'

Luke nodded, 'Okay.'

Steve pressed a button on the deck, and the large tape spools wound furiously back to the beginning of the song. 'Let's try it from the beginning,' he said into the microphone. 'When you're ready.'

Luke nodded once more, and moved back to the mike. The music floated through the control room.

Kate sighed. She couldn't see anything wrong with the way the song had been put together. She thought it sounded marvellous.

Luke's dark, melodic voice filled the room as he started to sing. Kate closed her eyes and leaned back in her chair. He really was a fantastic singer. She felt his voice spread ripples all over her body.

His voice was sexy, warm and earthy, fulfilling the promise of those dark good looks. The lyrics of the song were inspiring and the music lifted her.

She had been surprised to learn that Luke wrote, arranged and co-produced all his material. He really is a very talented man, she thought with a smile.

'Tired?' Janet's voice came from beside her.

Kate opened her eyes and smiled. 'We've been here for hours,' she said quietly. 'Why has he taken so long on just one song?'

Janet's brows shot up, her expression dry. 'Hours?' she chuckled. 'My dear, Luke has been known to spend a fortnight on just one song.'

Kate's eyes widened. 'A fortnight?' she repeated incredulously. She didn't realise he worked so hard. It was typical of her to suppose that just because

Luke Hastings was famous, he did absolutely nothing all day.

It was strange how one always assumed that the famous spent their days merely being famous, as though it was a full-time job. She felt rather guilty about being tired. If Luke could sing the same song over and over again without a break for four hours, the least she could do was listen, or try not to get restless.

For the next two hours Luke and Steve worked very hard, getting the song exactly right. One of the men who worked in the control room kept them supplied with coffee and stale biscuits. The room was filled with cigarette smoke, courtesy of the sound engineers who chain-smoked permanently.

At five o'clock Kate's eyes were watering and her limbs were cramped. She longed for a tub of steaming bath water and a breath of fresh air.

Steve's fair head was bent as he listened to the tape playing back. He pressed the red microphone button and leaned forward.

'Okay, Luke, I think that's about it for today. We can clear the loose ends tomorrow. It sounds great. All we need is the backing vocals, and we're on our way.'

Luke removed his gleaming headphones with a nod, and laid them down on the chair in front of him.

Steve leaned back in his seat and sighed with satisfaction. 'What do you think?' he asked Kate with a smile.

She inclined her head. 'I like it,' she said sincerely, 'but I don't think I'll buy it when it comes out. I know it backwards now!'

Steve laughed, and swung round in his chair. He turned his head to speak to the men behind him. 'Okay, you can start clearing away now. We're finished here for today.'

The men stood up, shuffling around the room as they put the spools of tape away, emptying ashtrays and throwing away coffee beakers.

Steve turned back to Kate, his blond hair glinting in the lights. 'Boy, do I need a pizza!' he said in an exaggerated New York drawl.

Kate laughed. The previous night he had told her in great detail about the all-night pizza houses in the city. Apparently he was a regular customer.

'We always go for a pizza after a hard day in the studio,' he said, glancing across at the other members of the production team, 'don't we, boys?' A chorus of agreement came from the other men. Kate saw something light up in Steve's eyes as he looked back at her. 'Hey, why don't you come with us one afternoon?' he asked.

Kate smiled. She hesitated before replying. She hadn't forgotten Luke's warning the previous night. But she saw only friendship in those warm brown eyes. Luke was making a fuss about nothing, she decided.

Steve took advantage of her hesitation and pressed on, 'We could go on a little tour of the city after we've eaten, kill two birds with one stone.'

Kate decided that Luke was likely to kill her with a lot of stones if she agreed. But she liked Steve. He seemed to be a nice man, even if he was a flirt. Besides, she compressed her lips determinedly, Luke wasn't running her life. He could jump off the top of the Empire State Building for all she cared.

'Thank you,' she said defiantly, 'I'd like that.'

Steve seemed pleasantly surprised for a second. Then he leaned across to her and stroked her cheek with a long, thin finger. 'Good,' he said, his eyes smiling at her, 'that's settled, then.'

Kate smiled at him warmly, then her eye was caught and held by Luke who had come in quietly and was now standing on the other side of the room.

His blue eyes glittered angrily between thick black lashes. His face was hard and controlled, his mouth compressed into a firm straight line. Kate saw the force in his body, the powerful unleashed anger, and shuddered.

He took a step towards them and Steve looked round, his hand falling away from her cheek.

'Hi, Luke,' he said cheerfully, 'I didn't see you there.'

Luke glanced at him, the menace in his eyes unhidden. 'I gathered that,' he said in a cold voice.

The other men in the room exchanged glances and looked at Luke, then at Kate, but didn't say a word.

Her cheeks began to colour furiously as she met their knowing stares. Luke had behaved as though she was his property. Now they believed the same as Janet did; they thought she was Luke Hastings' latest mistress.

'Are you both ready?' Luke's voice was clipped as he spoke to Janet and Kate.

After they had said their goodbyes to everyone in the studio, Kate and Janet followed Luke out to the waiting car. Janet nipped into the front, obviously suspecting that Luke and Kate were about to have an argument.

Kate sat beside Luke in an intense, angry silence. He didn't speak one word all the way back to the hotel, and she became more and more uncomfortable as the minutes ticked past. His presence was unnerving and her nerves were getting tangled up.

From time to time she glanced at him through her lashes, only to see his face set like a rock, his jaw thrusting out determinedly; his whole profile harsh and full of silent, controlled anger.

Janet excused herself discreetly when they arrived back at the hotel. She had notes to go over, she said, as she disappeared in the direction of the lift with a wry smile on her small lips.

'I'd better go up and help her,' Kate murmured hopefully, as she looked up at Luke.

His lean brown fingers curled painfully round her wrist, and she winced. Luke manoeuvred her into the bar without a word, his face flinty. He sat down in one of the plush armchairs beside a table, and Kate sat down too, rubbing her wrist ruefully as he released her. The waiter meandered over to take their order, and Kate watched him, silently wishing he would somehow contrive to stay until Luke had calmed down. The waiter left a few seconds later, reappearing with their drinks within moments.

Kate sipped her Martini, her nerves on edge as she waited for Luke to speak. She didn't think she could stand much more of his harsh, angry silence: it was like sitting on top of a volcano, waiting for it to erupt.

Luke flicked his eyes towards her. 'Have you deliberately set out to irritate me?' he asked, his voice as cold as ice.

She kept her face as bland as possible. 'I don't understand,' she murmured, her eyes cast down.

Luke's mouth shut like a steel trap. 'Don't play games,' he bit out, 'I'm not in a very playful mood.'

Kate jumped slightly at the angry undertones of his voice, even though it was lowered to prevent the other people in the bar hearing.

'Please don't shout,' she said quietly, keeping her eyes averted from his.

He leaned forward, his eyes glittering angrily. 'I'll shout as much as I damned well like,' he said, his voice clipped and lowered. 'Now tell me why you've deliberately gone against my instructions.'

Kate's mouth set in a firm, stubborn pink line, and she glared at him. 'Instructions?' she echoed through tight lips. 'Who in God's name do you think you are? Dishing out instructions to me as though I was your property!'

His face hardened. Kate had a feeling that if she tapped it with her finger she would feel concrete instead of skin and bone.

'I told you to stay away from Beck,' he said through his teeth. 'I might have known you'd spend all day flirting with him in the control room.'

Kate's fists clenched. 'I did not flirt with him all day! He spent the whole time working.'

'I suppose you didn't give him any encouragement either?'

'No,' she said tightly.

'Really?' His voice was sarcastic, one jet-black

brow raised unpleasantly. 'What was the meaning of that charming little scene I witnessed when I came in the room?'

She gritted her teeth. 'I was just talking to him,' she lied.

Luke gave a nasty laugh. 'I must be losing my touch! The permissive society moves too fast for me. I always thought touching was strictly for lovers. It seems it constitutes conversation now, too.'

'Why do you blow everything out of proportion?' she demanded. 'Why? You can never take anything at face value, can you? You have to read an ulterior motive into everything.'

'I use my eyes,' he snapped. 'I watched you both, remember. From where I was standing, you were giving him the green light. He was also stroking your cheek.'

Her eyes flashed angrily at him. He was deliberately reading more into it than there actually was. Apart from that, she didn't like his high-handed manner. She preferred to run her own life. She was damned if she would let him order her around!

'Steve was only being friendly,' she said. 'It's quite customary to offer friendship to someone who's a stranger in a new country.'

Luke raised one black brow. 'How kind of him,' he sneered. 'I must remember to thank him for showing such thoughtfulness towards my staff.'

'I am not a member of your staff!' she snapped.

'Don't be so bloody naïve. Who the hell do you think pays your wages?'

Kate sat back in her chair. She hadn't realised that Luke was actually paying her, she had thought

Janet handled that. But that still doesn't give him the right to order me about, she thought defiantly. If there was one thing she hated, it was arrogant men like him.

'I don't give a damn,' she said, standing up. 'If you expect me to obey orders like that you're out of your mind. You can take your job and shove it down a big black hole if you're going to start interfering with my private life!'

She turned and half ran out of the bar, leaving Luke staring angrily after her.

Dinner that evening was tense and unnerving. Kate kept quiet for the most part, speaking only when she was spoken to. She was still too angry to trust herself to speak to Luke. His attitude had been overbearing and small-minded.

She could see no earthly reason why she shouldn't accept Steve's offer. Luke was just being petty. He was behaving in a very dog-in-the-manger fashion about the whole thing. She had made it clear, she hoped, that she wasn't going to allow him to seduce her. No doubt that was why he was blowing up and overreacting over Steve's invitation.

The next day at the studio passed in much the same way as the first. Luke went over a new song for six hours, and Janet and Kate sat and listened patiently, becoming restless and tired very quickly.

Luke's stamina baffled her. He stood up all the time while he was recording, and his voice always sounded perfect. He never lost a note or forgot a lyric. He amazed her.

That evening they had dinner rather later than

before. The session at the studio had lasted until quite late. They had gone over and over the tapes, listening for signs of imperfection.

It was eight-thirty before they were all assembled in the bar. Steve was eating with them again.

'P.R., sweetheart,' he had told Kate. 'We always give Luke the V.I.P. treatment when he's here. When he gets fed up with seeing company representatives wherever he goes, he'll tell me to clear off.' He had glanced at Luke, a cheerful smile on his face, but the smile had faded when he encountered Luke's glacial stare.

Now Kate sipped her wine as a little silence fell over their table. She had spent most of the evening talking to Steve, mainly about all the places she had yet to visit in New York. Luke's presence was silently threatening.

Her mouth set angrily as she looked at him through her lashes. He had definitely put a damper on the evening.

'At least we have the afternoon off tomorrow,' said Janet, in an effort to break the uncomfortable silence.

Kate glanced at Luke. His face was like a rock. She really disliked him at that moment. Why did he have to be so difficult? She didn't understand why he felt obliged to place restrictions on her.

Suddenly she became aware of Luke's gaze as it was directed towards the doorway.

Slowly she turned her head, and her heart sank. Lisa Blair stood in the doorway. Her tall, slender body was encased in a long white fur, her flowing blonde hair a perfect foil against it. Beneath the coat was a glimpse of a tight-fitting black dress, emphasising her slim, model-girl curves. Long black leather boots set off the outfit perfectly.

Lisa swayed seductively across the restaurant towards them, and Luke stood up.

'What are you doing here, Lisa?' he asked bluntly.

Lisa reddened. 'Don't be rude, darling,' she said, her brown eyes narrowing into slits as she looked at Kate. She looked back up at Luke with a winning smile. 'I had some things to clear up at the Madison Avenue office,' she told him in a silky voice.

Janet raised an eyebrow. 'That's good,' she told her drily. 'Kate and I are going over there tomorrow afternoon. You can come with us.'

'Oh, I have to be there in the morning,' said Lisa. Kate suspected she had been a little too quick with that reply, but she couldn't be sure. Lisa seemed to exude confidence and glamour.

Luke's face was expressionless as he pulled up a chair for her. Lisa sat down, sliding out of her fur coat like an eel. She slung it carelessly over the back of the chair and crossed her legs smoothly, leaning back, her high breasts jutting out.

'Hello, Steve,' she murmured huskily. 'How's the recording coming along?'

'Okay, so far,' Steve said politely. He caught Kate's eye and winked, and Kate suppressed a smile. Something in Steve's face told her he didn't think much of Lisa. Well, that made a refreshing change, she thought as she watched the men in the bar turn and stare at Lisa openly.

Janet glanced at Lisa, her small red mouth pursed.

'Are you booked in here?' she asked.

Lisa nodded, her long blonde hair glimmering beneath the lights. 'Of course,' she said with a slow smile. She looked at Luke with smouldering eyes, lowering her voice to a husky undertone. 'I always stay where Luke is.'

Luke's hard mouth curved into a smile as he looked down at Lisa.

Kate felt something kick her viciously in the pit of her stomach. She looked away from them. I am not jealous, she told herself firmly, ignoring the sickening sensation spreading through her body.

Lisa looked at Kate. 'How are you, Katherine?' she asked. 'Are you enjoying this trip to America?'

Kate forced herself to turn her head and smiled. 'Yes. It's fascinating,' she told her politely.

Lisa smiled. 'Oh, I do agree,' she said in a voice like melting honey. 'So clever of you to get the job.'

Kate gritted her teeth and kept smiling. The waiter came over to their table as Luke crooked his finger, and Lisa gave him a winning smile, heightened when she watched his eyes pop out on stalks.

'Thank you, darling,' she purred to Luke, 'I really would love a drink.'

Kate wondered if she was going to ask for a saucer of milk. The waiter beamed at Lisa before whizzing off to bring her her drink. Why don't I ever get results like that? Kate wondered drily to herself, turning her head away from Lisa. She didn't think she could stand much more of this. Lisa had only been with them for fifteen minutes, and Kate was already trying to force down unpleasant feelings which were stirring all over her body.

Steve started up a conversation, fortunately, and Janet and Kate joined in eagerly. Kate felt another lurch inside her as she heard Luke and Lisa's conversation being carried in husky, intimate voices.

She glanced round. Her lips clamped together as she saw Luke, his black head bent, his blue eyes glittering down into Lisa's, his hard mouth curved into a sensuous smile as he spoke to her.

Kate looked at the clock, wishing time would fly. It plodded along slowly. Steve and Janet had now given up keeping her in the conversation. She sat silently staring at the clock, waiting for a convenient moment to excuse herself and go up to bed.

'Kate and I will be catching up on some paperwork tomorrow morning,' Janet was saying to Steve, her sharp blue eyes darting across to rest on Kate's face.

Kate looked up, smiling vaguely. 'Yes, we do have rather a lot to get done in the morning,' she agreed, glad she had caught the gist of what Janet had been saying.

'So long as she can keep her mind on her work,' Janet added with a slow smile.

Kate ignored that. Janet was too quick. Out of the corner of her eye she saw Luke and Lisa, still talking to each other quietly, and felt anger rise inside her. He had probably had Lisa flown out here because he sensed Kate wasn't likely to succumb to his seduction technique.

Luke caught her eye and smiled, his teeth white and strong against his tanned skin. 'Lisa's very tired,' he said, his voice dark and lazy as he stood up. 'Jetlag, I'm afraid.'

Janet raised a dark eyebrow, her sharp blue eyes resting on his face. 'We'll see you in the morning,' she drawled.

Lisa smiled like a Cheshire Cat as she looked at Kate. 'Goodnight, everybody,' she said.

Kate felt sharp stabs in her breastbone as she watched them walk away to the lift, Luke's lazy animal grace matched by Lisa's feline sway. He was so dark, so devastatingly attractive, and Lisa was the perfect blonde foil for his looks.

They look perfect together, Kate thought with a sinking heart, then pulled herself up sharply, pushing away the feelings she was experiencing. She tried to concentrate on what Steve and Janet were saying, but her mind kept throwing up images of Luke and Lisa. She felt sick, emotionally drained and very, very tired.

But the most disturbing factor was that she didn't know why she felt like that. She went to bed an hour later, and fell into a confused, restless sleep.

The next day she and Janet spent all morning making sense of the notes they had put together during their trips to the studio. Janet pottered about, grumbling because she couldn't find some missing notes. In the end, they were discovered behind the bathroom door in her bedroom. Kate didn't ask how they had got there.

They bypassed lunch in the hotel, deciding to go out to a restaurant on West 57th Street. Kate still felt very drained. Her mind was conjuring up images of Lisa and Luke spending all of the previous night in each other's arms. Every time she pushed her thoughts to one side, they came back with increased fervour.

Janet looked at her with understanding eyes while she spooned orange mousse into her small mouth.

'I think you can have the afternoon off,' she said with a smile.

Kate looked up. 'I thought that was all settled anyway?'

Janet shrugged. 'Luke's got an interview on this afternoon. The *Herald Tribune* are running a piece about him. I was going to ask you along, but you look like you need a break.'

Kate grimaced. 'That bad?' she asked quietly.

'That bad,' Janet nodded solemnly. Then she smiled. 'Don't worry, at least you won't have to put up with Miss Blair for a whole gruelling afternoon.'

'Is she going to be there?'

'I'm afraid so,' Janet chuckled. 'She likes to give the press the wrong idea about her and Luke.' She caught the expression of fleeting pain on Kate's face. 'Sorry,' she mumbled, pulling a face.

Kate was puzzled. She didn't understand the sharp attacks of jealousy she was experiencing. Luke means nothing to me, she told herself angrily as Janet dropped her off at the hotel.

Later, as she emerged from the shower, she decided to clear her mind completely of all thoughts of Luke. He was far too disturbing for her to spend hours dwelling on him.

The telephone rang; a short, buzzing sound, and Kate leant across the bed to answer it.

'Hello?' she said absently.

There was a pause. Then, 'Hi—it's Steve. How are you?'

'I'm fine,' said Kate, sitting down on the bed. 'How did the recording go this morning?'

'Great,' he assured her. He hesitated slightly before speaking again. 'Janet tells me you have the afternoon off.'

Kate smiled. 'That's right.'

'I have two tickets for the latest hit show on Broadway. How would you like to go?'

Kate bit her lip. She wasn't too anxious to encounter Luke's displeasure again. Then she remembered Lisa, and her lips tightened. If Luke could swan around with Lisa, she didn't see how he could possibly excuse himself for telling her off if she went out with Steve.

'Yes, I'd like that,' she said simply.

'Great!' Steve sounded exceedingly pleased with himself. 'Hey, why don't I meet you in a half hour and take you round the city before we see the show?'

Kate liked the idea. She would feel much safer exploring New York with a man by her side. 'Okay. I'll meet you in the foyer at three o'clock.'

She smiled as she finished dressing later, she was looking forward to being a tourist. She hummed a little tune to herself and picked up her bag. Steve was such lively and amusing company, she felt sure he would be able to bring her out of her previously gloomy mood.

Steve was waiting when she stepped out of the lift. He jumped up and came towards her.

'Like a drink first?' he asked.

She shook her head, smiling. 'Not really.'

Steve took her arm and led her out of the hotel. 'New York, here we come,' he quipped, hailing a passing taxi. Kate slipped into the back of the yellow cab, feeling excitement build inside her.

At last she was going to get a chance to see the city as she had wanted to do since she had arrived. She gazed out of the window happily, and settled back in her seat.

Steve took her on a whirlwind tour. She saw so many places, visited so many buildings, and talked so much to Steve that she was sure she should have forgotten Luke for the afternoon.

But his image seemed to be imprinted on her brain, and no amount of laughter could banish him. He hung over the afternoon like a black eagle.

Later, as she and Steve came out of the theatre on Broadway, Kate wondered for the hundredth time that day what Luke had been doing while she was out. No doubt he was entertaining Lisa, she thought miserably.

'We'll never get a cab here,' Steve told her after they had been waiting for twenty minutes outside the theatre. 'Let's walk uptown. We're bound to see one on the way.'

New York was still awake, although it was well past midnight. Neon signs lit the streets, flashing on and off constantly, competing with each other for the brightest light, the most dazzling colour.

Kate looked about herself with wonder. The same dynamic, burning energy was there as it had been during the day, only this time it was illuminated by hot neon, instead of the sun.

They finally hailed a cab and drove back to the

hotel. As they pulled up outside the vast glass doors, Kate turned to Steve with regret. The time had passed so quickly, even though Luke had been constantly on her mind.

'Thank you for taking me out,' she said with a warm smile. 'I've really had a wonderful time.'

Steve grinned cheerfully. 'It was my pleasure.'

Kate glanced at her watch. 'It's one o'clock in the morning!' she exclaimed incredulously.

Steve shrugged. 'That's not late. Besides, you won't have much work ahead tomorrow.'

Kate reached for the door handle. He put his hand on her arm, and she looked round slowly.

'Kate,' his voice was gentle, a slight frown marring his brow as he looked at her. He leaned forward in the dark cab, and brushed his lips against hers, then pulled her softly into his arms.

She tried to respond. She kissed him back gently, and put her arms around his neck. Why didn't anything happen? There were no tingles of awareness, no shivers of passion. Her heartbeat plodded along steadily.

Steve drew away after a while. 'No good, huh?' he said, his voice quiet, his smile wry.

Kate looked at him, her face anxious. 'I'm sorry, Steve.'

Steve stroked her hair. 'Don't worry about it,' he told her kindly. 'Sometimes it happens, sometimes it doesn't.'

She looked at him sadly. 'Steve . . .'

'Ssssh!' he placed a finger on her lips. 'I should have known you were someone else's property when I first set eyes on you. I told myself you weren't, because you and Luke hardly ever said a word to each other.' He grinned. 'I should have realised that when two people avoid each other's eyes all the time, there's got to be something there.'

Kate stared at him in amazement, her tired brain waking up instantly as she tried to grasp what he was telling her.

As she walked into the hotel foyer, his words echoed in her head. When two people avoid each other's eyes all the time, there's got to be something there.

Her heart sank to the ground as she went into the lift. She hadn't been able to understand her attitude towards Luke—the way she always knew when he was beside her, always felt herself knot up inside when he touched her.

Now she knew why she couldn't get him out of her mind. Now she understood those sharp pains she had felt when she saw him with Lisa.

She went down the corridor to her room, and opening the door, went in. She sat on the bed in the heavy silence and tried to come to terms with her feelings.

She was in love with Luke. She knew for certain now, knew she had fallen head over heels for him. She could have kicked herself till she was black and blue. What a stupid thing to do, she said to herself angrily. The worst person I could fall for!

The telephone rang, and she nearly jumped out of her skin. She leant across the bed and answered it.

'Hello?' she said.

There was a long pause. She heard someone breathing harshly, then there was a crash that hurt her eardrums as the receiver was banged down on her.

She frowned, looking at the receiver in her hand. Who on earth had that been? Fear crept into her stomach. A heavy breather? She shook her head with wry amusement. Now she was getting morbid!

She was just about to slip into bed when there was a loud hammering at the door. She picked up her negligee and went towards the door—then she bit her lip. What if it was a stranger, trying to force entry?

'Open this bloody door!' Luke's dark, angry voice dispelled any fears that it might be a stranger. But it replaced them with fears about letting him in.

'What do you want?' she asked, standing by the closed door.

Luke hammered on the door, and Kate jumped away from it nervously. 'If you don't open this door,' he said between his teeth, 'I'll break it down!'

Kate decided it would be better to let him in than have him break down the door, so she quickly opened it.

Luke's powerful body lunged through the door, and Kate backed away from him.

He slammed the door behind him. His face looked murderous. 'Where the hell have you been?' he demanded harshly.

Kate swallowed on a dry throat. 'I went out,' she said shakily.

Luke's mouth clamped shut. 'I know that,' he snarled, 'I've been ringing you every hour since eight o'clock.'

'Oh,' she said in a small, nervous voice.

'Yes, oh!' he snapped. He thrust his hands in his pockets and stood towering over her, looking down at her white face with rage in his eyes. 'Where have you been?' he asked.

She fidgeted with shaky hands, her fingers running along the edge of her negligee. 'I went to see a show on Broadway,' she told him.

'Who took you?'

She swallowed. 'Steve,' she whispered.

'I can't hear you,' he bellowed.

'Steve took me!' she yelled back, suddenly overcoming her nerves.

His eyes flashed angrily at her, blue sparks flying at her face. 'I might have known you'd sneak off with him the minute my back was turned!'

Her lips tightened. 'I did not sneak off with him!'

'No?' he asked unpleasantly. 'What do you call it, then?'

'I don't have to sneak anywhere,' she told him, 'I don't need your permission to go out. I'm not a child.'

'That is a matter for conjecture,' he snapped back. 'Where else did you go?' he demanded.

'We went around the city. We also had dinner.'

'Until one o'clock in the morning?' he sneered with disbelief. 'Come on, where did he take you?'

Her lips compressed into a thin line. 'I told you—to the theatre.'

'Don't try it on, baby, I'm not in the mood. Theatres close around eleven. What else did you do? Walk the streets eating hot chestnuts?'

Kate glared at him. 'Mind your own damned business!'

His hand shot out and gripped her wrist, and she winced in pain as his long fingers bit cruelly into her flesh.

'You cheap little tramp!' he breathed hoarsely, jerking her towards him. 'You've been giving him the come-on ever since you set eyes on him.'

'I have not!' she snapped furiously.

His eyes were almost blind with rage. 'No wonder I couldn't get you in bed! You can only turn on with skinny blond men.'

Kate sucked her breath in. Her hand flew up and connected with his face, and her fingers stung as she gazed in horror at the red marks on his tanned cheek.

Luke lifted his free hand slowly and touched his cheek, and Kate shrank away from the look in his eyes. She watched in mounting terror as his face contorted into a mask of pure rage, his skin taut across his cheekbones.

'I think,' he said thickly, 'I'm going to hit you.'

Kate opened her mouth and tried to scream, but nothing came out. His hands jerked her towards him, his fingers curling into her shoulders.

His eyes were like glowing coals as he looked down at her. Her negligee fell open, revealing the almost see-through blue nightdress. Luke looked at the marble-white skin of her breasts, noticing the way they moved up and down with fear, her heart hammering painfully against her breastbone. His gaze rested on her full pink mouth as it trembled, and she felt the searing heat of that gaze on her flesh.

'Oh, God,' he muttered hoarsely, his hands

moving down her back swifly, pulling her closer to him.

Her body was crushed against his as his mouth descended in a bruising, punishing kiss, and she felt as though she had stopped breathing, as her lips grated against her teeth.

Her arms were pinned to her sides, her hands curling as his powerful grip imposed itself on her body. She tried to struggle, but his arms were like a steel vice around her.

The kiss changed. His hot mouth moved seductively against hers, and flames ran through her body as she became aroused.

His long hands moved sensuously up and down her almost naked body, feeling so much through the sheer material of her nightdress. His thighs were hard against hers, his chest moving with his erratic breathing.

'Kate, Kate,' he groaned against her mouth, as he picked her up in his arms and carried her to the bed a few feet away.

Kate's mind reeled as she felt herself being deposited gently on the soft bed. She tried to get up, but his hands pushed her back, and his body moved to lie next to her.

Her heartbeat raced, her blood pressure shot up. One long hard thigh was thrust between hers, and his mouth returned to her lips with increased passion. She groaned huskily, her hands going up around his neck, her fingers twining in his hair.

Her breath caught in her throat. Luke's long fingers were moving over the flat plains of her stomach in a slow, burning motion. She arched towards him, her body melting with desire.

His hands closed over her high, pointed breasts and she gasped with pleasure. Her bones were quickly turning to liquid. She knew she was asking for trouble, she knew that she should push him away from her.

Her sexuality fought with her mind and won the battle hands down. She was pressing closer to him, her body shivering from head to toe with tingling excitement.

'Luke,' she murmured from deep within her throat, her eyes fluttering slightly as his mouth moved down to her neck.

His tongue flicked lightly against the soft skin of her throat, and she moaned with pleasure, her head moving restlessly from side to side.

Luke's body was hard against her, his strong hands moving dexterously across her soft skin. He released her aching breasts from the confines of the sheer lace nightdress and she thrust her head back, arching to meet him, needing to feel his mouth on her skin. She could feel his breath coming faster as it fanned her breast. Her nipples ached, hardening as her breasts swelled in his palm. His tongue snaked out across her nipple, and she gasped, her hands tangling in his hair as she writhed against him. His strong white teeth nibbled her softly shivering skin, inflaming her already molten desire.

His other hand moved softly, and she felt the long, hard fingers sliding up her thighs. She trembled, and sharp stabs of excitement ran through her. Her hands tightened on his head, pulling his hair as she felt her breath being dragged out of her.

'Kate,' he whispered close to her ear in husky

tones. 'Touch me,' he took her hand and placed it on his chest, holding it there firmly, 'darling, touch me.'

Her hand stroked his chest slowly. Her fingers slid between the buttons on his shirt, undoing them softly. His chest was hot, his flesh burning to her touch, and her fingers tangled in the crisply curling dark hairs.

She bent her head and pressed her hot mouth against his skin, her tongue snaking out across his flesh at the base of his throat.

Luke made a strangled noise in the back of his throat. 'Oh God, you're so beautiful,' he groaned, his hand stroking her thighs with fevered movements. His breath rasped in his throat, his heart crashed maniacally against the bones of his chest, hammering against Kate's hand. He pushed her back against the pillows, his eyes glittering down at her with naked desire. Her hair splayed out against the stark white of the pillow and her green eyes blazed with desire and love.

Luke's breath caught dangerously in his throat. 'Kate,' he whispered as he bent to kiss her, sliding on top of her, 'let me love you, darling.'

Kate's mind began to clear as she lay beneath him. His hands were gently stroking her, his lips dropping light kisses all over her face.

She loved him. She loved him more than anything she had ever known. But he was only making love to her because he wanted her for one night. He didn't want to love and keep her for ever.

He wanted her body, not her love. Pain flashed through her with white-hot intensity. She couldn't do it. She couldn't bring herself to let him take her, even though she loved him desperately.

Her passion cleared and she stared at him with agonised eyes, pain written all over her face.

'No, Luke,' she whispered, stiffening beneath him.

'I need you,' he murmured, his face hidden in the shadows, 'I need you now. Let me love you.'

She pushed at his chest. 'I can't let you do it,' she said, her eyes pricking with tears. He would never look at her again after this. He would never touch her again with those long, strong fingers, never kiss her again. But she just couldn't let her principles slide beneath her as easily as that.

Her eyes glittered as he looked up. 'What are you talking about?' he asked in a husky, slightly absent voice.

She bit her lip anxiously. 'I can't,' she whispered.

He stared at her for a moment, the desire in his eyes fading slightly. When he spoke, his voice was thick and controlled. 'Are you telling me that after all this, you're going to refuse me?'

The hot tears were blinked back as she gazed at him, her eyes agonised. 'I'm sorry,' she whispered painfully.

Luke swore viciously under his breath. 'You can't do this to me!' he said hoarsely.

Her hands gripped the sheets tightly. 'Don't get so angry,' she begged in a shaking voice.

'You little witch!' he muttered, his teeth exposed in a snarl. 'You teasing . . .' The rest was lost as he swore between his teeth.

Kate winced at his language. His face was full of rage, his eyes glittering dangerously, the skin across his cheekbones taut, showing white where the bone lay.

'Please, Luke . . .' she began anxiously, her face white with fear and pain.

'Shut up!' he bit out angrily, getting up from the bed, and doing his shirt up with trembling fingers. Kate watched him, her eyes filled with unshed tears.

'I'm so sorry, Luke,' she whispered in a choked little voice.

He looked at her, his face violent, unleased anger in every line of his powerful body. 'You're not sorry,' he snarled. 'I expect you're too bloody tired after spending all night in Steve's bed!'

Her hand flew to her mouth. So that was what he thought! 'No, Luke, it isn't . . .'

'I told you to shut up!' he said between his teeth, crossing the room to the door. He turned his black head, his eyes leaping with rage. 'I've never liked second-hand goods,' he said bitingly, and stalked out of the door, slamming it hard behind him.

Kate turned on her side, and the hot tears fell bitterly down her face as she cradled herself in her arms, rocking to and fro.

She had lost him. She had never had him to begin with. Now he despised her. Pain flowed through her body, and she closed her eyes tight, wishing she could wake up and find it had all been a bad dream.

She watched dawn approach as the pain dulled to a numb ache. She finally fell asleep at seven, full of abject misery and despair.

CHAPTER NINE

THERE was a very loud buzzing noise somewhere above her head, and she opened one sleepy eye and groped for the telephone receiver. Her head felt as though it had been padded with cotton wool and her throat was dry.

'Hello?' she mumbled, propping herself up on one elbow.

'Good morning!' said a cheery American voice. 'This is your early morning call. It is now one minute past eight o'clock.'

Her eyes closed momentarily. 'Thanks,' she muttered, replacing the receiver back in its plastic cradle.

She crawled out of bed and padded across to the bathroom. Her legs had the feel of rubber, and she almost stumbled into the door of the shower. She leant wearily against the sink, and raised her tired eyes to look in the mirror. Her face was white and blotchy, her eyes ringed with red from crying. The tip of her nose was slightly pink and sore. She pulled a face at her reflection, and undressed quickly, stepping into the shower.

The water cocooned her in a warm, safe sanctuary which she was reluctant to leave. Her mind wandered uncontrollably to the previous night. Luke's angry face flitted into her mind's eye, his bitter, violent words echoing in her ears.

There was very little she could do to make him change his mind about her. He obviously thought she was a scheming little tramp. It hurt her to realise that that was what he thought of her. She had never done anything to deserve that opinion. Perhaps if he spoke to Steve—but no, that would never work. Luke would only ignore the truth now.

People only believed what they wanted to believe. Luke had formed his opinion, and he wasn't likely to go back on it.

She stepped out of the shower and wrapped a large, fluffy bathtowel around herself. She splashed ice-cold water on her eyes, trying to ease the redness, but it didn't do much good. Her eyes looked as though she had bumped into a lamp-post.

Hunting through her case, she found a pair of dark glasses she had packed on a wild impulse. She slipped them on and looked hopefully into the mirror. They made her look a little out of place, but at least they disguised her swollen eyes.

She tied her hair back in a black silk scarf, and dressed in a pair of tight-fitting black trousers, a black silk waistcoat and a white blouse. She left the buttons on the waistcoat undone, and looked once more into the mirror.

She grinned suddenly on a wild bubble of almost hysterical mirth. All I need, she thought, is a trenchcoat and I'll look like a gangster's moll!

She walked to the door with her bag in her hand. The corridor was deserted. She walked down to the lift, and waited nervously, stepping in with relief when it arrived.

Two stout German men stood in the lift, talking

rapidly in their own language. They fell silent as Kate went in the lift, and looked at her appreciatively. She ignored them, and they soon began talking again.

Perhaps she could speak to Luke, get him to see he was wrong. It niggled her that he should hold such an opinion of her. It also hurt her very much. At least he doesn't know I'm in love with him, she thought, her eye on the red numbers as they approached the ground floor.

She could be grateful for that at least. Would it make any difference to him, to know that she loved him? The lift doors slid open and she stepped into the foyer.

Her heart leapt convulsively into her throat. Her pulses thudded in her wrists, her ears, her throat. Her hand clutched painfully on the handle of her bag as she forced herself to walk forwards.

Luke stood in the centre of the foyer with his back to her. His black hair curled crisply on his collar, and she wanted to reach out and run her fingers through it. The formal black suit he wore emphasised his tall, powerful body. Her eyes flowed over his broad shoulders, and on down to his long, long legs. A faint sense of longing filled her and her knees went suddenly weak.

He turned around, aware that he was being watched. Icy blue eyes cut through her like a blast of cold air. His hard mouth was compressed into a thin, straight line, and his face was like a rock, as though it was carved from granite. His eyes glittered like a thousand steel knives, and Kate shivered.

Now that she was actually facing him, she found

she couldn't bring herself to just walk past him. She felt a sudden urge to talk to him. She wanted to take his arm and force him to listen to her.

She knew this was going to be her only chance of getting through to him. If she left it for another time, she would be coming up against an impenetrable wall. If she didn't attempt to speak to him, he would only take it as an admission of guilt.

She took a deep breath and walked forwards. As she came closer, she saw the icy contempt in his eyes and winced. But there was no turning back. This was her last chance, and she was grasping it with both hands and clinging on tight.

'Luke . . ' she began huskily, her voice shaking with nerves. But he merely gave her another look of scathing contempt, and turned his head away from her. She bit her lip worriedly. 'Luke,' her voice was trembling and uncertain, 'I want to speak to you.'

But he didn't turn around. She laid a hand on the dark material of his sleeve. Her fingers curled gently on his arm, trying to attract his attention.

The black head turned slowly. His thick black lashes were still as they rested against his tanned cheek. The blue eyes were icy. He looked at her for a long moment, and she felt the blood in her veins turn to ice. She shuddered.

The contempt in those eyes was unmistakable. He despised her. She looked deep into those icy blue eyes and felt herself dying very slowly, her heart contracting painfully as she realised she had blown her last chance.

Her hand fell away from his arm. Luke looked at her for another long, cool moment, his hard mouth straight, his face harsh and enigmatic. Then he turned away without a word, leaving her standing alone as he walked slowly out of the hotel.

Tears blurred her vision, as she turned and stumbled back to the lift. She leant against the mirrored panel as the lift took her back up to the fifteenth floor. Tears trickled out from under the lenses of her dark glasses.

She wiped them away with a shaky hand, sniffling like a child. She couldn't stay here. She was so tired of crying, so tired of the tension which had always surrounded her and Luke. Now the tension would be worse. It would kill her to have to watch him day after day, seeing the hatred in his face.

She packed in her bedroom, wiping tears away blankly as she stuffed all her clothes in the case in a haphazard fashion. She had to get out. Go back to England. Go home.

Home. She hugged the word to her, feeling the warmth and security envelop her. She would have to look for a new job, of course. She would also have to find a flat.

Her world darkened further. There just didn't seem any way out of it. A tear slipped over her cheek and into her trembling mouth. What the hell did she care? It didn't matter that much. She was so tired of it all. She just didn't care about anything any more.

She rang the desk and asked them to get her a taxi, scribbling a quick note to Janet telling her that she had to leave immediately. Then she left the note at the desk and climbed into the waiting yellow taxi with a sigh of relief.

The journey to the airport was long and tiring. Kate sat back, watching New York City change into New York County as the streets flashed by with painful clarity. The pain pulled at her with every inch they drove. She was never going to see Luke again. She would never hear that dark, lazy voice, never taste his kiss or look in his eyes again.

Try to keep him out of your mind, she told herself firmly. He despised her, and she would just have to face up to that. She would have to begin again, get a new job, a new flat, make new friends. Forget.

They pulled up outside the vast glass sliding doors of the airport, and Kate stepped out of the car, feeling the muscles in her legs ache from the journey. She paid the driver his exorbitant fee and went into the terminal building.

She walked on unsteady legs, through the departure lounge, her eyes searching desperately for the blue, white and red uniform of the ground staff of the airline she wanted to use. She spotted the desk and went over.

'Can I help you?' The girl sitting behind the desk looked up, her beautiful face heavily made up with expensive cosmetics. Kate wondered how many bottles of perfume she had used that morning as she smelt the almost overpowering scent which hovered around the girl.

'Do you have any spare seats on a London flight today?' Kate asked politely.

'One moment,' the voice was a refined American accent, 'I'll check for you.'

She tapped the computer keyboard in front of her with long, slim, red-tipped fingers. Her heavily made up eyes stared for a moment at the reading on the screen in front of her.

'We can give you a seat on the one o'clock flight,' she said with a polished, artificial, air-hostess smile.

Kate took out her cheque book and wandered over to the bank to get some cash. The price of the ticket was very high and would make a very large black hole in her savings. But it was worth it as far as she was concerned.

'Your flight will be called at twelve-twenty,' the girl said with another smile as she handed the ticket to Kate a moment later. Kate thanked her and walked away to deposit her luggage.

She sat in the cafeteria an hour later with her fourth cup of murky coffee. Drinking coffee kept her hands and her mind occupied. The stuff was disgusting, however, and looked like mud.

A young man dressed in jeans sat opposite. He had a large metal tape recorder by his side, which he played loudly, ignoring the angry glances he got from passers-by who objected to the music.

'. . . Don't cry out loud . . .' sang the girl on the cassette, and Kate bent her head, trying to ignore the strident voice and poignant lyrics, Luke's face floated into her mind. She saw the deep blue glitter of his eyes as he bent his head to kiss her, then the vision faded.

'. . . if you should fall, remember you almost had it all . . .' sang the girl on the cassette, and Kate's hand shook uncontrollably as she lifted her coffee cup to her lips. Her heart moved with the raw emotion in the girl's voice. She stood up and left the cafeteria, trying to get away from the memories the music evoked.

The clock on the wall ticked slowly. She sat and watched it as the digits moved closer to twelve-twenty. She checked her passport for the hundredth time with nervous fingers.

The impersonal voice on the loudspeaker told her that her flight was being called. She felt her heart thump in slow motion, a desperate sad rhythm. The yellow light of passport control loomed ahead of her. She walked towards the barrier in a daze.

It was then that she heard the voice, and stopped in her tracks.

'Kate!'

She kept on walking. It's your imagination, she told herself firmly.

'Kate! Stop!' The voice was urgent now as she reached the barrier. She turned around slowly, not wanting to see what she feared. I'm going mad now, she told herself, hearing voices all over the place. They'll tie me up and burn me at the stake like Joan of Arc.

Luke was running across the departure lounge towards her. His thick black hair lifted slightly as he ran, his black cashmere overcoat flying apart, his long, powerful legs carrying him closer.

Kate just stood silently watching. Her heart was moving like a frantic butterfly. Why was he here? How had he found out? Was he going to stop her leaving, or accuse her of some new crime?

He reached her then, and stood in front of her, breathing hard. His face was strained, his eyes searching hers, trying to see behind the dark lenses she wore.

'Why are you here?' she asked in a tight voice.

Luke towered over her, his dark head bent as he studied her intensely. 'I came to apologise,' he said roughly.

She watched him. What had caused this sudden change of heart? Her head tilted to one side, waiting for him to speak.

'Last night,' he said slowly. His eyes dropped to the floor, as though masking an emotion he didn't want her to guess at. 'Kate,' he said thickly, pausing to look back up. He raked a hand through his black hair. 'Kate, I'm sorry. I shouldn't have behaved the way I did. I had no right. I was wrong. I was half-crazed, I couldn't think straight.' The words were spoken in a clipped, breathless voice, with an underlying thread of tenderness.

'What made you change your mind?' she asked coldly.

He grimaced. 'When we arrived at the studio, Steve said something about your evening out, and I went crazy. I went for his jugular vein like a madman, and the boys had to pull me off. Steve was shocked. He told me I was an idiot, in so many words. He said you were in love with me, not him, and if I couldn't see that, I was a fool.'

Kate looked at him bitterly. The colour rose in her cheeks. 'Steve had no right to say that. It's none of his business.'

'Kate, I'm sorry about what happened last night.' His voice was quiet, his face intense. 'But I couldn't stand the thought of another man with you. I went berserk, imagining you in Steve's arms. I knew you'd been out with him because the hotel porter saw you together. When you came back and admitted it, I wanted to kill you,' he grimaced, 'literally.'

'I thought you would for a moment,' Kate admitted. 'I was frightened.'

Luke's black head bent slowly, and his lips brushed against hers in a soft and brief kiss. He drew away, and raked a hand through his hair. Kate watched him silently. He was trying to think of the words to explain to her.

'I nearly went crazy, I wanted you so much. I thought I was going to explode with it. But when you said you'd been with Steve, I wanted to kill you. Then it all got tangled up somewhere along the line, and I couldn't keep my hands off you. I couldn't help myself. I really needed you. When you refused me—my God, I thought my head was going to blow up! It took every ounce of will-power I had to get off that bed and leave you alone. I went to my room and had a few stiff drinks.'

Kate shook her head. The loudspeaker was booming once more, announcing that the flight was closing at gate seventeen. She looked at Luke with tired eyes. He was watching her intensely.

'I have to go. They'll be boarding in a moment,' she told him in a quiet voice. All he had told her was that he wanted her. It was as she had suspected; he only wanted her to be his mistress. The pain of that thought cut through her. It would be harder for her to bear than not seeing him at all.

She smiled sadly, and turned. Luke's hand caught her arm, and he pulled her back to stand in front of him.

'I can't let you go, Kate,' he said huskily.

Her lips tightened. Who the hell was he kidding? He could have his pick of any woman who would be glad to be his mistress. But not her. Oh no, she wouldn't let him do that to her. She had too much self-respect for that.

She looked pointedly at his hand. 'Let me go, Luke,' she said quietly.

His hard lips firmed into a straight line and his eyes flashed with an emotion she couldn't quite grasp. 'No.' His long fingers slid around her waist, and he pulled her towards him. He pressed his mouth against her hair. 'I love you,' he murmured in an urgent voice. 'I can't let you walk away from me. I want you to stay with me for ever. I've never felt like this for any woman before, and now that I've found you, I'm not going to let you go.'

Kate felt a shock wave of happiness run through her. She didn't know whether to laugh or cry. She drew back and looked at him in wonder. Was he being serious? Or was this yet another ploy to get her to surrender?

Luke looked down at her. 'If you don't love me now,' he said in a dark voice, his face hard and expressionless, 'I'm sure you'll grow to love me in time. I'll make you happy, I promise you.'

Kate laughed softly. 'I do love you,' she whispered huskily.

His tanned face relaxed, a smile curving his hard lips. He reached out a hand and deftly removed her glasses. 'How can I talk to you when I can't see your eyes?' he said as he took them off.

His breath caught in his throat, and Kate felt herself blush furiously. He studied her swollen eyes with seeming wonder, then a smile curved his mouth, his white teeth vivid against his skin.

'You've been crying,' he said, running one long finger over her red eyes. His voice sounded incredulous and pleased.

Kate's lips tightened as she saw the mirth in his eyes. 'What's so funny?' she asked crossly.

Luke shook his head. 'I'm sorry, darling, I'm not laughing. I'm just pleased.'

'Pleased?' she echoed. 'Pleased that I've been crying?'

Luke looked sheepish. 'It shows you care,' he explained. 'I wasn't sure. I thought perhaps I meant nothing to you. I thought I didn't stand a chance after last night.'

She smiled, much against her will. A large bubble of happiness was currently churning her insides as she gazed deep into Luke's dazzling blue eyes. There was real warmth and tenderness in those eyes now, and her heart leapt as she looked at him.

'Kate,' he murmured gently, his face coming closer. His mouth covered hers in a slow, burning kiss, his hands pulling her softly against the length of his body. Her hands tangled in his hair, holding him as tightly as she could. She was afraid that if she let go, he would disappear.

A light flashed in the airport lounge and they pulled apart, and Kate blushed as she met curious pairs of eyes. A reporter and photographer headed the crowd of people. He grinned at them.

'Could we have another shot like that, Mr Hastings?' he asked in a cheerful nasal voice. 'One of you kissing your cousin?'

Luke looked angry for a moment. The blue eyes narrowed, his mouth tightening, then he looked at Kate and smiled.

'She's not my cousin,' he told the photographers. 'She's my future wife.'

Kate felt her heart stop. Would she be able to cope with the pressures of his fame? How would she react if she saw his name wrongly linked with another woman, merely to get good copy? She felt herself smile inside. She knew how the papers twisted things all out of proportion. She would stand by Luke, help him, be with him, believe in him and above all, love him.

She looked into his eyes, and felt her heart glow with happiness. She would be able to take the pressures of being his wife. She knew that. She knew it because she loved him deeply, needed him desperately, and wanted to stay by his side for ever.

'If you'll have me, of course,' Luke murmured huskily in her ear, a little smile playing around his lips.

Kate nodded, unable to speak because of the lump in her throat. Her answer lay in her eyes, and Luke smiled as he read it.

The flashbulbs popped furiously as Luke's black head bent to take her mouth again, and Kate surrendered to his kiss in delirious ecstasy.

A WELSH BOMBSHELL

The people in the Welsh town of Pontypridd can well remember years ago a four-year-old boy standing on an orange-crate stage on street corners singing his heart out. Little did they know that this boy, whose name was Tom Jones, would some day break international box-office records for his performances in the world's greatest concert halls.

Tom Jones was discovered singing in local pubs in the coal-mining district of Wales. Eventually Jones was taken to London's Tin Pan Alley, given a song to record, and "It's Not Unusual" climbed to number one on the British hit parade in 1965.

But Tom Jones's deep rich voice is only part of the reason for his popularity. His darkly handsome features, coupled with a body toned by hours of daily exercise, have given him a stage appearance that has caused thousands of female fans to forget husbands and boyfriends, and throw perfumed scarves or hotel-room keys onto the stage!

Jones's first hit song marked the start of his meteoric rise to stardom and was followed by other tunes, such as "Green Green Grass of Home," "What's New Pussy Cat?" and "Delilah." He also hosted a network television show in the United States and was the first performer to break the color barrier in South Africa by insisting on performing to mixed audiences.

Now, at the age of forty-two, a more mellow Tom Jones continues to tour. Women still adore him, and Tom Jones doesn't mind at all. "I want people to feel relaxed and this seems to make them feel good," he says. No wonder he's one of the world's most popular singers!